# Old Money

Gerald Brence

# OLD MONEY

### GERALD BRENCE

ISBN: 979-8-9880718-9-1 (Paperback)

Printed in the United States of America

Published by

QUIPPY
QUILL

info@thequippyquill.com
(302) 295-2278

# CONTENTS

# CHAPTER ONE

The old Johnson County bridge was a terrifying site. There it was, right in front of us. It was a hunk of gray, decaying wood and metal that stretched a good fifty yards across the Kansas River. The structure sagged in the middle at an angle that made your heart sink. The wooden tracks grabbed most of your attention.

Drivers had to hit them just right or risk sliding into the water. There were no side rails for protection. And of course, the bridge creaked like a rocking chair when the wind blew.

A hundred feet below was the river itself. It was muddy and black. The three of us just stared at it, but nobody said anything. It was me, Hayden Lewis, who had gotten us into this mess, so I needed to think of a way to get us out of it.

"It just looks scary." I said it like I was even trying to convince myself. "If we stay on the tracks and go slow, we'll be okay."

Maybe I sounded like I had a lot of confidence, but in reality, I had none. I was scared to death. There was no way I was going to drive that old pickup truck across the bridge. On top of that, we were pulling a trailer full of cattle. I needed one of those other two boys to do it for me.

Johnny Suggs was a scrawny kid with a big mouth. He said what he wanted to say, and he never backed down after he said it.

Riley Archer was big and thick-shouldered. He stood nearly a foot taller than Johnny and a half a foot taller than me. He didn't talk much, and he rarely smiled. It seemed to me that he was mad about something.

Our job that summer day was to haul thirteen head of cattle from a farm near Olathe, Kansas over to another farm about ten miles away. We would travel through the back roads of Johnson County. Halfway between the two farms hung the bridge.

We were working for a man named Mr. Clinton Derryberry. I was a city kid from Olathe who didn't know anything about farming or hard work.

Mr. Derryberry spotted me in the barber shop a few Saturday afternoons ago. He was stepping down from the chair as I stood next in line.

"I need a hand just about like you," he said. "You looking for a job, Boy.

I never had a job before. I was only thirteen. I also had never spent much time around a grown man. My dad passed away when I was little. School had just let out for summer, so I thought it was a good idea.

"Sure," I answered, "I could use a job."

That little conversation in the barber shop would change my life forever. Mr. Derryberry was a nice man, but he only paid three dollars an hour. That was the going rate in 1973. It didn't take me long to understand the truth about physical labor. I figured out fast that getting somebody else to help me do all the work was a good idea. Plus, it got lonely working out on a farm.

On the third day of my employment, I brought the subject up to Mr. Derryberry. "This is a lot of work," I stated. "Three good hands would be a lot better than one, and it would only cost you nine dollars an hour." Mr. Derryberry took his straw hat off with his left hand and rubbed his chin with his right hand. Soon he was nodding his head.

"Hayden," he said, "you're pretty smart. That's what I like about you." A couple of Saturdays later, Riley Archer showed up to work. A week after that Johnny Suggs appeared. Mr. Derryberry found them down at the barber shop, too.

My confidence in wheeling and dealing started to grow. Then one day I went a little too far. There is more work than can ever be done on a farm, and Mr. Derryberry was farming a lot.

We were behind on everything, but those cattle had to be moved. There was nothing left in the pasture for them to eat.

"Mr. Derryberry," I said, "me and those two boys can take the cattle over to the other pasture. I can drive!"

Mr. Derryberry was a little astounded.

"You can drive?" he questioned me.

"You don't have no driver's license, do you Boy?"

I decided to go for it.

"Sure, I can," I answered. "Let me show you."

It was easy for me. My mama taught me to drive a long time ago. I convinced him that I could do it in ten minutes.

The two other boys jumped in the front seat with me and away we went.

At that point, we didn't even know each other's names. Nobody said a word until we got out of Mr. Derryberry's site. Then suddenly, Johnny Suggs broke the ice.

"Watch out, Kid!" he screamed out of the blue.

"You're gonna get us all killed!"

I slammed on the brakes. The trailer crunched into the back of the pickup.

The cattle mooed and hollered. Johnny Suggs laughed like a hyena. Riley Archer growled. I tried to compose myself.

Slowly and surely, I continued driving.

After a couple of miles, Johnny did it again.

"Look out for that snake, Kid!" Once again, he screamed out his laughter, but this time I kept on driving.

I was going really slow. I was startled and scared, but it was important that I didn't show him how much he was bothering me.

We drove on a good way, and Johnny Suggs talked the whole time.

"How would you like to have a name like Derryberry?" he asked. "I'd run away if I was him. I bet his first name is Harry. How 'bout that name, Harry Derryberry?"

He laughed so hard that he had to lean over and hold his stomach.

I glanced over at him and frowned.

Riley Archer didn't say a word. He just looked straight ahead.

"Old Harry's so fat," Johnny continued,

"I bet he can't see his private parts over his belly button!"

Just as soon as he said that, I turned left. At first, I didn't realize how intimidating the bridge looked. But as we got closer, I was stunned. I shut down the truck and pulled on the emergency brake. My eyes were as wide as silver dollars.

Riley Archer opened his door and got out of the vehicle. Johnny Suggs was right behind him. I sat in the truck for a while.

"What in the world had I gotten us into?" I thought to myself.

"Come on, Kid," Johnny yelled at me.

"Get out of the truck!"

He and Riley had made it to the foot of the bridge. It took me a few minutes to get my wits together. By then, Johnny Suggs and Riley Archer had gotten into an argument.

"The Kid ain't got the cahoonies to drive across the bridge," Johnny said.

Riley finally spoke. "Yeah, he does. You just need to shut your trap, you little Runt. I'm already sick and tired of listening to you."

Johnny Suggs retaliated at the insult by trying to hit Riley. However, Riley stuck out his left arm, and he put it on Johnny's forehead. That stopped him cold. Johnny couldn't even reach him.

Finally, Riley pushed him aside and walked back to the truck.

"Hey, Kid," he said, "are we gonna go across the bridge or what?"

"I don't feel so good about driving across," I said quietly to Riley Archer.

"What if we put the truck in neutral and pull it across? There's a big tow rope in the back."

"Hey, Runt!" Riley hollered. "Kid says that we should pull the truck across with a tow rope. What do you think?" Johnny Suggs never hesitated.

"That's a good idea!" he yelled. "You can do the pulling. You'd be a good Mule.

That's probably all you're good for."

For some reason, he thought that was really funny.

"Shut up, Runt!" I yelled.

By then, all three of us were getting used to the verbal abuse.

"Hey, Mule," Runt continued, "you see this rock I got in my hand here?"

Both of us looked at him. For a second, we thought he was going to throw the rock at us.

"I bet I can throw this rock further than you. Get over here and let's see." Mule turned around and walked back down to the bridge. He picked up a rock about the same size as the one Johnny Suggs had in his hand. He wound up and tried to throw it across the river. It landed several feet short and splashed in the water.

"Shoot!" Johnny Suggs howled.

"What a sissy!"

In one step, Runt fired a fastball. The rock hit the water and skipped to the other side. It was an impressive throw.

I walked over to join the competition.

For the next hour, we threw rocks across the river.

That was how it all got started. From then on Johnny Suggs' name was Runt.

We called Riley Archer, Mule. My name was Kid.

# CHAPTER TWO

After that, the three of us would look for places to meet, so we could hang out together.

One central location for the three of us was the junior high basketball courts in the middle of town. That was where all the guys would be, big and small, young and old. Three on three pickup basketball games started there early in the day and lasted all the way until dark.

One day we met there after school.

Runt was the only one of us who could actually get out there and compete with the bigger guys. Mule and I could barely handle the ball, much less shoot.

However, if we got in line and waited, eventually we would get our chance to play. When we got our chance, we played until a challenging team beat us.

That was how it worked.

There were some serious bullies there.

One guy in particular named Tom

Wayne Rhyner ruled the courts. He was in high school. We were barely in junior high. He was big, tall and muscular. We were just a bunch of snot-nosed kids. It was obvious that he didn't even know we existed.

As we waited and watched the action, Tom Wayne insulted and intimidated everyone he could. His team won every game. Finally, our time came. The three of us slowly crept out on the court.

Everybody knew it was going to be a slaughter.

"Hey, Kid!" Runt yelled to me. "Take the point."

I didn't even know what that meant.

It didn't matter. Runt threw a bounce pass right at me. I missed it and had to chase the ball all the way to the fence.

Everybody laughed as I endured my humiliation. The game started. Tom Wayne Rhyner stole my first pass and took it behind the line. He passed to his teammate.

The teammate passed it back to him.

With the confidence of a pro, Tom Wayne went straight to the basket and slam dunked right over Runt. The goals were only nine foot tall.

Tom Wayne grabbed the ball and fired it right at Runt's head. It knocked him down. The ball bounced away again.

This time nobody noticed me retrieving it. They were all watching what would happen between Runt and Tom Wayne Rhyner.

"You boys need to go home and change your diapers!" Tom Wayne yelled.

All the other kids laughed. The game was called "Make It, Take It." That meant as long as you kept scoring, you always kept the ball. You had to make a defensive stop to get possession. Tom Wayne took the ball to the point at the top of the circle, and his team scored again. Pretty soon we were down by five baskets.

That was when Mule stepped up. He was not a good basketball player, but he hated being embarrassed.

"Let me guard him," he said to Runt.

He was referring to Tom Wayne Rhyner.

Immediately, the game became very physical. Mule couldn't stay with Tom Wayne's quick feet, but he could get in position to block him from the basket.

He didn't worry about fouling, and Tom Wayne didn't like that.

"Get off me, you Punk!" Tom Wayne whined.

Suddenly, he threw an elbow that connected into Mule's cheek bone. That was when things escalated.

Tom Wayne made an easy layup. I could feel the tension from the other side of the court. Mule was just staring at him.

"You think you're something?" Tom Wayne yelled at Mule. "You think you're bad?"

Mule kept staring at him. In a flash, Tom Wayne went after him. Mule was a big kid for junior high, but he was no match for Tom Wayne Rhyner.

Tom Wayne threw his arm around

Mule's neck and got behind him. Mule had no chance. In a matter of seconds, Tom Wayne had him in a choke hold.

He started walking him down the middle of the concrete basketball court.

Everybody watched in horror.

Mule fought bravely, but he was way overmatched. Tom Wayne was choking him and swinging him from side to side. He was also screaming some loud war hoop as he was doing it.

Just then, the darndest thing happened. Out of nowhere, Runt came running full speed at Tom Wayne who had Mule in a headlock. He hit Tom Wayne with his shoulder so hard it knocked all three of them to the ground.

To this day, it was the best tackle I've ever seen!

It took a few seconds for all three of them to react. Runt made it to his feet first. He stared at Tom Wayne. Mule just watched.

Suddenly, Runt took off running. Tom Wayne Rhyner started chasing him.

None of us knew what to do, so we started running behind Tom Wayne.

Tom Wayne Rhyner was the biggest, fastest athlete in the whole town.

Surely, he would catch Runt and beat the crap out of him. Or so it seemed.

The chase went up one street and down the next. Soon, people started dropping out. They couldn't keep up.

Runt ducked under shrubs, jumped over fences and ran like his life depended on it, because it probably did!

Tom Wayne was right behind him the whole way.

Runt ran and ran and ran. Tom Wayne never stopped chasing him.

Runt skipped across the railroad tracks and down behind the cotton gin. He thought he had escaped, so he took a break to catch his breath. When he peeked around the corner of the gin, he was terrified when he saw that Tom Wayne was standing thirty yards away looking for him.

Runt knew where to go, so he took off again. Tom Wayne spotted him and came running as fast as he could.

Runt turned the corner onto Linwood Street and headed for his house. His lead was shrinking. Tom Wayne was close behind him.

"I hope the front door isn't locked!" Runt thought to himself.

Fortunately, the front door was open.

Runt hit the front porch, opened the door and entered his house. As quickly as he could, he locked every door and hid in the bathroom. No one in his family was there.

Tom Wayne Rhyner hit the front porch and grabbed the door handle. He was going to go right on into the house, but he couldn't get in. He pounded on the door with his fist. It didn't matter to him that he damaged the screen door.

After scanning the property, Tom Wayne finally gave up.

"I'll get you, you little Punk!" he screamed. "You better watch your step!"

Tom Wayne Rhyner turned and walked away. A few seconds later, Runt gathered up enough courage to go look out the front window. He watched Tom Wayne Rhyner walk away. His heart was beating so hard he could hear it.

# CHAPTER THREE

Runt lived on the north side of town. Mule lived over on the east side. I lived down south.

If it weren't for Mr. Derryberry, we might not have ever even met. But after working together on the farm for a few days, we found ways to run into each other.

Runt loved baseball, and he was always making plans for us to go to games. One day we met down at the old American Legion complex. They had the only field big enough for the high school team.

We made our way down to the dugout, so we could be close to the players. Runt seemed to be in awe of them. We were sitting right on the edge of the bench, obviously in the way. Guess who walked right up to us? It was Tom Wayne Rhyner.

"You punks need to get up in the stands," he said. "You don't have any business being down here with the men."

Runt responded in an instant. "The game hasn't started yet," he yelled. "You can't make us leave."

Tom Wayne Rhyner was the biggest guy on the team and the best player. He was also pretty much universally hated by everybody.

"What's your name, you little knot head?" Tom Wayne asked.

"My friends call me Runt!" He said it proudly.

Tom Wayne scowled at him. "Well, I don't like you Runt, so get out of here!" I'll never forget the look on Runt's face. He didn't seem scared of Tom Wayne Rhyner. He was just undersized, humiliated and embarrassed. So much for looking up to a high school role model. Runt stared him down as we walked away.

Soon, we started meeting at a high school in the middle of town. A bunch of the older boys would play this silly game called "Run Through Tackle." It was an easy game to understand. One kid got out in the middle of the huge grass field in front of the school. When the game started, kids would run from one end to the other end. If the guy in the middle tackled you, then you were on his team. That's when you had to start tackling guys, too. When only one person was left in the game that wasn't tackled, he was the winner.

You can imagine what kind of a player

Runt was. He taunted everybody, whether he was on the running side or the tackling side. Of course, he was especially hard on Mule.

One day we got to the school as a game was getting started. Tom Wayne

Rhyner was in the middle of the field.

He was enjoying punishing the older kids. He only tolerated the young kids like us. We weren't even welcome in the game.

"Hey, Tom Wayne!" Runt screamed on his fourth trip across the field. "You're so ugly when your mama dropped you off at school, she got a ticket for littering."

Runt thought he was really funny, but Tom Wayne never gave him any attention at all. He was too busy trying to make a tackle.

So, Runt took off running on his fifth trip. He was quick and could make a sidestep in a flash. He would wait on Tom Wayne to turn around, and then he sprinted right up to his back.

Suddenly, a quick turn would get him out of trouble.

Runt waited on Tom Wayne to turn his back again, then he took off on his sixth trip. This time he was really brazen. He ran right up under Tom Wayne's right arm and veered away. As he jogged to safety, he held his arms out to his sides to imitate an airplane. That was his signature move, but Tom Wayne Rhyner didn't seem to notice. I have to admit that I was getting bored. Mule had tripped and fallen down. He was in the middle trying to tackle, but he was having no success.

The older guys, including Tom Wayne, were focusing on people their own age.

They didn't care about us. It was easy to run across without being threatened.

There wasn't much of a game to it.

Runt walked over to me. He wanted to talk.

"Kid," he said, "Mule ain't much of a ballplayer, is he?"

I didn't pay any attention to him, because Runt always talked like that.

I jogged out to the middle of the field.

When I got about ten yards away from Mule, I slowed down to a stop. It only took him a few seconds to tackle me.

Now both of us were with all the other guys in the middle. All of a sudden, things started picking up.

Runt flew by me. "Wake up, Kid!" He screamed it as loud as he could.

As Runt finished his seventh trip, he laughed. "This is a record!" he yelled.

"Seven trips and you boys ain't even touched me. We're gonna be here all day!"

By then all the runners were on one side of the field. Suddenly, about half of them took off, but Runt stayed back.

Mule and I started trying to get tackles.

We were fighting for our pride at that point. We could hear Runt yelling way down at the other end.

"Here comes my world record, eight trips across the field. You guys better get ready!"

But Runt didn't realize that Tom Wayne Rhyner was waiting for him on this trip. When Runt came running up on him, Tom Wayne turned to his left. All he had to do was stick out his arm. His elbow caught Runt right in the mouth. I swear Runt's feet flew up over his head, and he landed flat on his back.

Everybody stopped to see the carnage. Runt was lying on the ground screaming. He had both hands cupped over his face. I ran over to him.

"Runt, are you okay?" I asked.

He just kept on hollering and screaming. Finally, I grabbed his hands and pulled them back. Everybody backed away. It looked like a bomb had gone off in his mouth. His front teeth were gone. Quickly, I put his hands back over his face.

Tom Wayne Rhyner just stood there.

He wasn't in a hurry to leave. He looked down on the both of us. "Well, Runt," he said. "I guess eight ain't your lucky number, huh?"

# CHAPTER FOUR

The school principal picked up runt and took him to the hospital.

He was a wreck. Having false front teeth for the rest of his life was gonna be a reality.

His mom didn't take it too well. After she heard the story, she was pretty mad at Tom Wayne Rhyner. She was mad at all of us. There was no money or insurance to pay for dental bills.

I remember sitting at the hospital when Mr. and Mrs. Derryberry walked in the door. I never knew how they found out about Runt's teeth. Mr. Derryberry seemed angry. Mrs. Derryberry seemed concerned. She stayed with Runt's mother the whole time.

Mr. Derryberry scowled at me and Mule when he walked by us. He never said a word as he walked straight back to see the dentist. That was when I advised Mule that he better just go on home. Without showing any emotion, he got up and left.

An hour passed before Mr. Derryberry re-entered the waiting room. When he saw that it was just me by myself, his mood seemed to change. He sat down.

"You boys," he said, "you need to be more careful. Runt's teeth won't ever be the same."

We sat there for the next hour. Neither of us said a word, but I could tell that Mr. Derryberry was kinda enjoying it. It was giving him a chance to be a daddy.

It was awkward at first, but I could tell how much he really cared.

Finally, Runt walked out of the emergency room with his mother and Mrs. Derryberry. He had his head tilted back. Both of his eyes were black and swollen shut. He didn't acknowledge me as he walked by. His mama had hold of his elbow and was leading him out the door. I looked away when she eyeballed me. Mrs. Derryberry scooted right along behind her.

Mr. Derryberry wanted to hear the whole story. I did my best to explain what happened without being a rat, but he saw right through my line of nonsense.

"Kid," he scolded, "I expect you to always tell me the truth. Now I need to know. Did Tom Wayne do it on purpose?"

"Well, Sir," I explained, "I'm really not sure. Now that's the truth. He just "There have been other kids who have got hurt," I said. "I bet they're playing it right now back over at the school." I never saw Mr. Derryberry in my whole life that he wasn't either wearing or carrying a straw cowboy hat. His bald head had a few small hairs growing out the top. He was a big man. I would say he weighed over two hundred fifty pounds easy. A big wart stuck out on the left side of his nose. Of course, Runt made fun of the wart all the time.

It seemed like we sat in that waiting room forever. There was no reason for us to even be at the hospital. Runt, his mother and Mrs. Derryberry were all gone. Finally, Mr. Derryberry was ready to lecture me. At least that was what I thought.

"Kid," he started, "I've been thinking." At that moment, it struck me funny that he called us by nicknames instead of our real names. The thought hit me that he was just one of us.

"I think the world of all three of you boys. You know that."

For a second, I thought he was gonna cry.

"But," he stopped talking for a few seconds. "From here on, I'm gonna just talk to you about business. Do you understand what I mean?"

I had no idea what he meant, but I nodded my head anyway. I wanted to go home.

"Kid," he started again, "when I want you boys to do something, I'm gonna just tell you. Then, you can tell Runt and

Mule. Things will work a lot better that way. It's a better way to do business." I have to admit. I wasn't paying close attention. I heard what he said, but I wouldn't say it really registered with me. I just nodded my head again. Mr. Derryberry smiled.

"Thanks, Kid," he said. "I feel better now. I have been wanting to have this talk with you. I just wish it was under better circumstances."

Mr. Derryberry got up and walked over to the receptionist. He pulled a big checkbook wallet out of his back pocket.

He placed his hat on the floor. I never saw him wear his hat indoors.

"We need to settle this bill, ma'am," he said. "I will pay it."

I sat in my chair and watched him.

After he was finished, he walked back over to me. He was very serious.

"Kid," he said, "I know that accidents are gonna happen, but I expect you to solve these disputes. Do you understand?"

I hadn't been focusing on what he was saying early in the conversation, but I was now. It was understood that was my first order from Mr. Derryberry in our new agreement. I needed to attempt to fix this feud between us and Tom Wayne Rhyner.

Another thought ran through my mind. Runt wasn't going to be making fun of Mr. Derryberry anymore. I was going to make sure of that myself.

# CHAPTER FIVE

Time went by, and things got better. But it still didn't stop Runt from being ornery anytime he could. After all, that was his act.

Then, all of a sudden, a new fad hit the country. People were taking off all their clothes and putting on some kind of a mask. Next, they would run around naked. It was called "streaking." Of course, that was the kind of fun that Runt loved.

All three of us were already sick of our hometown, even though we weren't old enough to have a driver's license. Runt always used to say, "You gotta be bad to have any fun around here."

He taught us how to do it one Saturday night after the movie let out. We walked over to the local drugstore to buy some ice cream. There were about thirty or forty people milling around town. They were mostly young couples. Almost all of the people our age had gone home.

Mule and I weren't paying very close attention. Runt snuck off and went behind the building. We were sitting out on the front sidewalk when all the excitement started. First, it was a few high-pitched laughs. Next, all kinds of hollering got started. Neither Mule nor I understood what was happening.

Suddenly, we both noticed a short little person running through the city square naked. His arms were stretched out to make it look like an airplane was landing. He made a "whoop" sound with his voice. We were startled. At first, it didn't register with me who it was. His body was not impressive.

It dawned on me to look at his face, but he was wearing a clown mask.

It was one of those masks that had the little band that stretched around the back of his head. That's when I remembered that Runt used that mask last Halloween.

The streaker made a left turn at the corner and quickly decided to take a lap around the courthouse. He was running fast, really fast. Finally, he ran out of sight. We never saw him again that night.

Monday at school I confronted Runt.

"Runt," I said, "You're crazy. What if you would have got caught?"

Runt looked at me. "What are you talking about?" he asked.

I turned my head away and rolled my eyes, "I'm talking 'bout you running around naked through downtown the other night."

"I did not, Sir!" he responded. "I would never do anything like that."

That was when I learned that never admitting to streaking was going to be part of the gag. I never heard Runt confess to it.

A few weeks went by, and it started getting cold. School let out for Thanksgiving holiday. On Wednesday night, we all got together downtown.

Runt had found a place where we could play pool. None of the three of us had a daddy, or we wouldn't have gone there No self-respecting rather would allow his son to go into a place like that.

It cost a quarter to play a game, but there was a lot of gambling. Guys would put their quarter down to get in line.

They would also put what money they wanted to bet on their pool skills. Runt pulled out a twenty-dollar bill and set it next to his quarter. I have to admit that I was a little awestruck seeing that.

After a few games, Runt's money was next in line. All of a sudden, the door swung open. Guess who walked inside?

It was Tom Wayne Rhyner himself. He wore a cowboy shirt that was cut off at the shoulders. I remember his bulging biceps scared me.

"So, you want to play for those twenty dollars, Boy?" Tom Wayne asked the question as he cut in line.

It was pretty obvious what the answer was gonna be.

"Sure," Runt replied. "Game on, Brother!"

I had never heard Runt say "Brother" before. Tom Wayne pulled a wad of cash out of his pocket. It didn't take him long to find a twenty-dollar bill to put on the table.

Runt and Tom Wayne went at it. I was standing by the jukebox watching.

Tom Wayne took the lead, but Runt caught up fast. Suddenly, Tom Wayne made a comeback. Right before he got ready to shoot the eight ball into the corner pocket to win, everybody started hollering.

I was pretty focused on the pool shot.

I didn't see the naked man running through the room. This time the streaker was big and stocky. He was wearing a gorilla mask. Tom Wayne tried to shoot anyway, but he was distracted. The streaker ran right by him before heading out the door and into the street. He had his arms stretched out and was acting like an airplane was weaving through the sky.

Tom Wayne seemed distracted. He missed the shot.

Quickly, Runt aimed his pool stick and started to shoot. Tom Wayne had left him with an easy shot to knock in the three balls. The only ball left was the eight ball. Runt tapped it into the side pocket. The game was over.

The excitement caught everyone's attention. I stood back at the jukebox.

Runt stood at the pool table. Tom Wayne glared at him. There was money all over the table. Either one of them could swipe it all up and take off, but neither one did.

The hollering got louder. The streaker had run around the block and was back in front of the hall. One of the pool players took off his shoe and threw it at him. The shoe hit the naked man on the shoulder.

Runt stuck out his chest and walked over to pick up the forty dollars. Tom Wayne stepped over to confront him.

Suddenly, I decided to spring into action. I got between the two of them and faced Tom Wayne.

"I'll play you a game," I said. "Come on, rack 'em up."

I glanced back to find Runt, but he was gone. There was no sign of him. Tom Wayne took off out the door to chase him. By now, all kinds of people were outside looking for the naked man, but he was gone, too.

Everything had happened so fast. I didn't know what to do, so I just started walking home. About halfway there I remember smiling. I felt pretty good. I had figured out a way to contribute to the team.

# CHAPTER SIX

Mr. Derryberry was trying really hard to get into the oil service business. He had some limited success as a farmer and a rancher, but he was interested in getting a bigger piece of the action.

Finally, he landed a job. It was simple.
All we had to do was run a big tube from a water pit out to the pasture. It was only about two miles long.

Mr. Derryberry summoned me to his big, white Ford pickup truck early on a Saturday morning.

"Kid," he said, "we got an oil field job today!"

I could tell he was really excited. He commenced to instructing me on what to tell Runt and Mule to do. I was to drive and haul them in the old Ford work truck behind him to the job.

He also told me that I was to be the foreman. He would supervise, and we would execute the job. I never told Runt or Mule about me being the foreman.

It only took one day to complete the work. We were very careful to do everything perfect. After all, it was our first job. Mr. Derryberry decided to throw in a makeshift fence that circled the water pit. He wanted to make sure that we got more work in the future. He didn't have to do it, but he had plenty of materials from the farm. His other motivation was to teach us how to build a fence. Fence building was going to be a big part of his oil field business.

We finished the job at around four o'clock and headed back to the farm.

When we got there, the work truck was full of useless leftover materials from the job

"Kid!" Mr. Derryberry yelled. "Drive that truck to the dump and get rid of all that trash. I don't want this property to look messy."

"Yes Sir, Mr. Derryberry," I answered.

Me, Runt and Mule got in the pickup and headed into town. It was about ten miles away. As soon as we got out of sight, Mule started complaining.

"I never get to sit behind the wheel," he whined. "How come you always get to drive?"

Well, I didn't have anything against Mule driving, but Runt couldn't help himself.

"Why if you drive, we'll all probably end up gettin' keeled," he ranted. "I ain't riding if you're gonna drive."

That was an opening for me. I would have loved to watch Runt walk all the way back to town, so I pulled over and put the truck in neutral. I stomped on the emergency brake. "You're up, Mule!"

I shouted.

Mule and I jumped out of the truck and ran around to change sides. Runt sat in the middle seat. Mule had never driven a vehicle, but he had been watching. He stepped on the clutch and pulled the "three on a tree" gear lever into first.

He stepped on the gas, but he forgot to release the parking brake. The truck jumped, rocked and roared. Runt was laughing so hard. I thought he was gonna choke.

Mule gathered his wits and released the brake. We took off again. At first, he drove really slow like an old lady. After a few minutes, we started moving down the road at a decent pace.

Things were going well. Everything got quiet. Then suddenly, Runt couldn't contain himself any longer.

"Watch out!!!" he yelled.

Mule slammed on the brakes and turned to the right. We slid right into a ditch. All kinds of trash fell out of the truck.

That was when I remembered what Mr. Derryberry had told me about keeping the peace. To tell you the truth, I was scared of Runt and Mule. I just got out of the truck and started picking up the trash. Runt and Mule sat and watched me until I was finished.

"Let me sit in the middle, Runt," I said.

I got in there and taught Mule how to drive. We didn't have any more trouble 'til we got to the dump.

We pulled into town and made our way over the landfill. Mule was doing a good job as the driver. We pulled up to the window. The door opened, and who walked out, but Tom Wayne Rhyner.

As soon as he saw Runt, he got mad.

The scowl on his face was obvious. Tom Wayne walked around the truck and gave it a good inspection. Finally, he walked over to the driver side window.

"You got a driver's license, Boy?" he asked Mule.

Of course, Mule didn't have a driver's license. He wasn't old enough, so he just told the truth. "No," he said. "I ain't got no driver's license."

Tom Wayne didn't stop there. "You got a electricity bill?" he asked. "You have to have a electricity bill to dump trash in here, you know."

Mule didn't flinch. "No," he answered.

"I ain't got no 'electricity bill, either."

Tom Wayne smiled. We all noticed that his teeth were half black from cavities.

"Then you just turn your ass around and get out of here, Boy," he said.

I could tell Mule was mad as an old goat. Runt was over by the window snickering.

Mule put the truck in gear and slowly turned around. I noticed that he was looking in the rear-view window. Tom Wayne was having himself a big 'ole time with the other dump workers at our expense.

Just as we were about to exit the premises, Runt decided to chime in on the conversation. "He hates you, Mule.

He wants to kick your butt. Come on, you can take him. Don't be a peon." Suddenly, Mule stopped and stepped on the emergency brake. He got out of the truck and headed back towards Tom Wayne. Runt got out on the other side.
"I was only kidding, Mule," he shouted.

"Get back in the truck!"

But it was too late. Mule was headed straight towards Tom Wayne Rhyner, and it was gonna get ugly.

I got out of the truck to watch. Mule kept walking. Tom Wayne was laughing and bragging. "You think you're tough, don't you Boy?" he shouted. "Come on over here and take your ass whoopin'!"

Mule walked straight up to Tom Wayne and punched him right in the mouth. I swear it knocked him flat on his back. Mule turned around and started walking back towards the truck.

Me and Runt stood there in amazement.

Tom Wayne got up off the ground. "I'll kill you, you punk!" he screamed. He started running right at Mule.

When he got about ten yards away, Runt yelled, "Look out!" Mule turned around to his left and socked Tom Wayne in the mouth again. Tom Wayne stumbled backwards a few steps and fell down. This time, he didn't get up at all.

Mule was as calm as he could be as he walked back to the truck.

"Come on," he said. "Let's go."

We drove out of the dump and turned right. After we drove about twenty-five yards, Mule stopped the truck again. He got out and walked to the back. He started grabbing the trash out of the bed of the truck, and he threw it over the fence into the dump yard.

Very slowly, me and Runt got out to help him. When we were done with our littering, we got back in the truck and drove away.

Suddenly, it hit me. "What in the world is Mr. Derryberry gonna say about this?"

# CHAPTER SEVEN

Mr. Derryberry took the news a lot better than I thought he would. He didn't like Tom Wayne Rhyner either. The mayor called him personally and told him about the incident at the dump.

Everybody in town knew everybody else's vehicles, so there was no secret about who owned the truck. Tom Wayne was the mayor's son. That was why he had a job at the dump.

I never knew what the ramifications were of us throwing trash onto city property. Mr. Derryberry didn't tell us.

He kept it between himself and the mayor.

All I knew was that Mr. Derryberry gave Mule a choice. He could either be out of a job, or he could attend church three Sundays in a row with himself and Mrs. Derryberry. I guess he thought they could help him get some religion.

For some reason, Mr. Derryberry didn't say a word to either me or Runt about it, but Mule told us all about it.

Mule said he balked at first, but he finally agreed. By then, I think he would have done anything to keep his job, so he could hang out with me and Runt.

The incident sparked Mr. Derryberry to start lecturing us. At least, it was kind of like a lecturing. He just started telling us what he thought about things.

"Do everything in threes!" he would say. "That way you know when to start, stop and take a break. Plus, you will start seeing results to what you're doing."

"Try to use your downtime effectively." That was another of his favorites. "Sitting around doing nothing is wasteful. Make sure you are always doing something productive.

That's how you learn."

Then, there was my favorite. He always made a big deal out of loving your job.

"I never saw a good farmer who didn't love farming! You can't be a good school teacher if you don't love to teach!" In other words, make sure you enjoy whatever job you choose. Riding around listening to his stories all day often made us wonder if he realized we didn't like working on a farm like he did.

Mr. Derryberry didn't just tell us once.

He would tell the same thing over and over. I guess he thought it would eventually sink in on us, and that was how he did it.

The big day, Sunday, rolled around.

Runt decided that we should hide out and watch, so we got up early to meet downtown at the First Methodist Church. We hid behind the bushes across the street. It was easy to spot Mr. Derryberry's big, white Ford truck driving towards us.

We skipped along behind cover to get in position to see him park. Quickly, the Mr. and Mrs. got out of the truck.

They both seemed to stand and wait for something. Finally, the back door opened, and Mule stepped into the street. His hair was combed, and it seemed that he was wearing clean clothes. Runt started giggling.

They started walking away from us towards the church. That was when Runt did the rudest thing that I ever saw in my life. He picked up a rock and threw it like a baseball. It hit Mule right in the middle of the back. Mule turned around and scowled, but he couldn't see us.

A few seconds later, he started walking towards the church again. As soon as he did that, Runt fired another rock. This one skipped on the sidewalk and hit Mrs. Derryberry smack in the rear end.

I was so embarrassed that I was a part of this sin I couldn't stand myself. If I could have made a run for it, I would have done it. But I couldn't do that.

Everyone would have seen me.

I got down on my belly and peered through the bottom of the bushes. Mrs.

Derryberry was looking around like a hawk searching for a rat. I could tell that she was really mad, but she seemed to shrug it off and headed back to the church.

Now there are some guys who just can't ever seem to get enough, and Runt was one of those guys. He raised up and threw another rock. This one was way off target, though. It bounced into the yard by the church.

He got down on the ground and started snickering like he always did when he thought he was going to get away with something. But he had a surprise coming. Mrs. Derryberry turned around and started walking straight toward us. I guess I was a coward. I started scrambling on all fours sideways around the bushes and escaped.

Runt panicked. He couldn't believe Mrs. Derryberry would come after him, and he just froze on site. She walked straight to him.

"Runt," she said, "you get up off that ground right now. Do you hear me?"

Runt got up like a scared dog. Mrs. Derryberry grabbed him by the left ear and started pulling him towards the church. I was in shock as I watched the four of them walk straight in the door.

I didn't know what to do. The church bell rang. The other churchgoers entered. I laid down on the ground and played possum. With one eye, I looked through the bushes.

About five minutes passed. Suddenly, one of the wooden doors opened, and a man appeared. It was Mr. Derryberry.

He put on his hat and started looking around. He didn't stay outside for very long. He had to get back into church. I could tell he was frustrated and angry. I knew he was looking for me.

# CHAPTER EIGHT

High school days are bittersweet.

At least that was what I experienced. Once we started into our junior year, Runt wasn't a runt any more. He was almost six foot two, and he was skinny as a rail. I bet he didn't weigh one hundred fifty pounds.

His hair turned bright red, and his lily-white skin was full of freckles.

Mule's physique was just the opposite.

He was shorter, about five foot ten, and stocky. There was no question that he was the strongest kid in school. Nobody ever messed with him. He still didn't talk much, and you knew when he did say something that he meant it.

My body was about the same as always. I was just a regular guy who had no exceptional skill. I was shorter than most of the other kids, and I was probably lower than average in courage.

It was all I could do to hold my own at anything.

One night when we were all really bored, things changed forever. That was the first night that we ever got into alcohol. It was Runt's idea to bribe Mule's sister, Twyla, into buying us some Mad Dog 2020 wine down at the liquor store.

I'll never forget the negotiation process that night. Runt and I made our way over to Mule's house at 6:00 p.m.

We knew his mama had gone to play Bingo. Twyla didn't have a date that night. She was pretty homely looking, and we knew that she didn't have any money. It was the perfect opportunity.

Runt knocked on the door and waited for Twyla to answer. He winked at me as we waited. At the time, I had no idea what he was up to.

When she made it into the house, Runt started executing his plan.

"Twyla," he started, "what do you have planned for tonight?"

She seemed to be in a pretty good mood, so she answered quickly.

"A couple of friends of mine are coming over to the house. I think we might go to the movies."

"Do we know any of them?" Runt asked. "Maybe we can all go together."

That last statement caught me and Mule off guard. "Maybe we can 8°

together?" That was the last thing either one of us wanted to do. Mule sure didn't want to hang out with his sister, and I had no interest at all.

Of course, Runt knew that. He also knew that Twyla had no intention of spending her Saturday night with three renegade teenage boys, either. That was why he kept prodding along.

"What's showing?" he asked.

Twyla started to seem a little perturbed.

"A movie called Steel Magnolias," she responded. "It's a chick flick. You wouldn't like it."

But Runt was way ahead of her.

"Steel Magnolias!" he shouted. "I've been wanting to see that! We can all sit together! It will be fun!"

By now, me and Mule were really getting nervous. Twyla started making her way back to the kitchen.

"I don't want to go to a movie!" I all but screamed.

Runt elbowed me in the rib cage.

When I looked up at him, he scowled at me.

Mule was watching the Cardinals and the Cubs play baseball on TV. Runt and I settled in with him and waited on Twyla. It only took a few minutes until she surfaced again.

"What time does the movie start?"

Runt asked her.

Her reaction stated the obvious. She was not interested in us accompanying her. There was no verbal answer.

"I heard they have some good popcorn at the movies, and I like Dolly Parton." I could tell that Twyla was about to panic. How in the world would she explain to her friends that her teenage brother and his two awful friends were going to attend the movies with them?

It just wasn't an option.

That was when the conversation turned a little sour.

"You guys are not going to the movies with us," she said. "You three can go do your own thing tonight without us."

Runt put the sad look on his face before he spoke again.

"Well," he said after a few seconds, "I'm going to the movies and sit behind you girls whether you like it or not." Things were getting tense. "No, you're not," Twyla answered.

"Yes, I am," Runt responded.

It quieted down for a few minutes before Twyla spoke up.

"Forget it, Runt. My friends and I are not interested in spending the evening with you."

Runt shook his head and looked at his watch.

"What time will the girls get here?" he asked. "I bet the movie starts at 7:30 or so. They'll be here in a few minutes, won't they?"

That was when I could see the panic in Twyla's eyes. It was obvious that Runt had his mind made up. I looked over at Mule. He had no interest in getting involved in his sister's quarrels.

Twyla walked over to the couch and sat down across from me and Runt.

She had a very serious look on her face.

Finally, she spoke.

"Runt, I'm serious. You can't hang out with us tonight. Please just leave us alone."

Runt looked at her and smiled. "Well," he said, "if you're interested, there is something else you could do for us.

If you do it, we won't be going to the movies with you."

# CHAPTER NINE

Runt had heard about mad Dog 2020 from an oil field hand that we had worked with out in the field. It turned out to be a bad choice. Twyla went down to the liquor store and bought two big bottles for us.

It was my idea to pay her $20 for her trouble. I figured we might need her to do it again someday. There had to be something in it for her, or why would she bother?

The party was down at the local park.

Nobody ever went there but us. At least that was what it seemed. We went to the swing sets and sat on a bench. I kicked it off by pouring a big draw into a glass Mule had bought at the State Fair.

We were all three rookie boozers. I remember the taste of the cheap wine just twisting my face, but I didn't show it. That would be a sign of weakness.

Mule seemed to be a natural drinker.

He went easy and slow, but he drank more than any of us. He used a foam cup.

Runt slugged big gulps right out of the bottle. Every time he took a swig, he would yell, "Woo Hoo!" It was grating after a while.

Before long, the rowdy behavior began.

Runt decided that he wanted to see how high he could swing. He went way up in the air. Suddenly, he decided to jump out of the swing at the highest point.

When he landed, he grabbed his ankle.

We ran over to him.

"I broke my foot! I broke my foot!" he screamed.

Mule had no sympathy for him. "You deserve it!" he yelled. "You always got to play the fool, don't you?"

Mule went back to his foam cup. I went back to my State Fair glass. Runt rolled around a while, then he got up and limped over to us. He had only sprained his ankle a little bit.

Pretty soon, the supply of Mad Dog 2020 was getting low. It was time to go do something. We headed to the pool hall. When we got there, Runt tried to play a few games, but he couldn't even hit the ball square. Once he missed a shot so bad the pool cue tip hit the carpet on the table and almost tore it.

Mule got a big kick out of that.

"Runt," he said, "you got a little too much torque on that one, didn't ya?"

Mule was drinking a Coke out of a bottle. He was standing at the bottom corner of the table closest to the bar. All of a sudden, he dropped the bottle. It crashed and broke into pieces. The dark, wet, gooey liquid smothered the floor.

The man who owned the pool hall jumped all over him. "Mule," he scolded, "now you get to clean that up. Get over here and get the mop."

Mule took the mop and put it against the wall. He got down on his knees and started picking up the broken glass. As he soaked up the Coke with a towel, I noticed that he started meddling with the leg piece of the pool table. He was down there for at least thirty minutes or so. I almost fell asleep waiting on him. The Mad Dog 2020 was starting to get to me. I couldn't help but laugh when Mule bumped his head on the table as he tried to get up off his knees. We were all pretty drunk. Everybody was having a good old time when the mood suddenly turned sour. Guess who walked in with his entourage? It was none other than Tom Wayne Rhyner.

Tom Wayne had aged gracefully, but he was still cocky, mean and always looking for a fight. Somehow, Runt and Mule knew he would be at the pool hall.

That was why we went there. Things started slow. There were no greetings exchanged. It was Saturday night, so most people were focusing on drinking, not playing pool. It just so happened that Runt had control of the table when Tom Wayne slapped down his quarter to challenge. He also put down a $50 bill.

Runt took his fists and rubbed eyes.

Mule and I were watching close. All of a sudden, he reached into his pocket and pulled out some cash. He put two twenties and a ten on the top of Tom Wayne's money. The game was on again.

I must explain how a teenager like Runt had that kind of money. It was because we had been working for Mr.

Derryberry. He had given us a raise that was a little bit above what the going rate for labor was at the time. We were now making $6 an hour, and we worked lots of hours.

Mr. Derryberry was also great at keeping up when we got into overtime pay. Sometimes, he nudged it our way a bit. Mule, Runt and I always noticed. Mr. Derryberry was very smart. He knew how to build loyalty. It seemed like we always had money in our pockets, probably too much money.

Runt was wobbling as he broke the rack on his first shot. None of the balls went into a pocket. Tom Wayne commenced to sinking three stripes before he missed.

Slowly, Runt started catching up. It took me a while before I noticed that he was almost always shooting balls into one corner pocket of the table. It was the same corner of the table where Mule had dropped the Coke bottle.

The game went on and on. I realized that Tom Wayne had probably been drinking too, or he would have won the game easily. Runt was playing terrible.

After a few minutes, only one ball was left on the table. That was the eight ball. Whoever sank it would win. Tom Wayne went first and missed. Runt went next and missed. He left Tom Wayne with an easy, easy shot. All he had to do was sink the eight ball into that same corner that Runt had been shooting at the entire game. It was a gimme.

Tom Wayne couldn't help himself. He smiled at Runt. "Well," he said, "I knew you couldn't handle the pressure. You're not just a Runt. You're a punk, too." Runt was too drunk to respond. Tom Wayne stepped up to shoot. He tapped the cue ball, and it tapped the eight ball.

The eight ball went in first, then the cue ball rolled in right behind it. It was a scratch. Runt won the game by default.

Mule walked over to the money that was lying on the table. He picked it up and put it in his pocket. That was a smart move on his part, because everybody in the pool hall knew that a brawl was about to break out in just a few seconds.

# CHAPTER TEN

I didn't find out until a few days later that when Mule dropped the Coke bottle on the floor and broke it to pieces, he also turned the knob on the pool table leg. That lowered the corner of the table, so Runt could cheat against Tom Wayne Rhyner in the bet.

At first, it made me mad. Mule and Runt seemed to like to keep me in the dark when they teamed up for mischief.

I didn't understand why they didn't let me in on their secrets. I guess they both thought I was too honest or something.

When Tom Wayne scratched on the eight ball, he went into a rage. I don't think he knew the table was tilted. He was just mad that Runt had taken it to him again.

I thought he was gonna take his pool stick after Runt, but that never happened. Tom Wayne just dropped the stick and grabbed him by the throat.

Runt wasn't much of a fighter, but Mule sure was. As soon as Tom Wayne started the action, Mule came in and knocked him off of Runt. That was when things got crazy.

I helped a little bit, but I started looking for an exit plan. Runt had to protect his false teeth, so he kept his fists over his mouth. That resulted in him getting two black eyes that night.

He got punched out by one of Tom Wayne's buddies while Mule boxed Tom Wayne. Soon, they got into a wrestling match. Neither one of them got hurt much, and I escaped with no injuries.

There was only one police officer on duty that night. His name was T.J. Middlebrooks. Everybody in town knew T.J. We all liked him, and we didn't want to bring him into our affairs. It was his hollering and threatening to throw us in jail that got us to stop fighting.

I think T.J. was sure glad that we responded in peace, because I could tell he was worried that nobody would pay attention to him.

After everything calmed down, T.J. took us straight to the police station to call our mothers. He wasn't sure if we were old enough to be in the pool hall or not. The discipline would be handed out by family members. That was the way it was done. At least that was what he thought.

After making the phone calls, T.J. came out of his office in a panic. None of our moms were at home. It was Saturday night, and they had other things to do.

T.J. pulled up a chair and looked at us. We were a mess. My shirt was torn so bad it was barely hanging on my body. The side of Runt's face was bleeding. Mule's hair was standing up straight. That was when Officer T.J.

Middlebrooks threw the three of us a curveball.

"Don't you boys all work for Clinton Derryberry?" he asked.

We all stared straight ahead. Nobody knew what to say or do, so we didn't say or do anything.

"Yeah," T.J. answered for us. "You boys work for Mr. Derryberry, don't you?"

He stood up and puffed out his chest.

Yeah, he figured that he had got us on this one. He knew Mr. Derryberry a little but not a lot.

T.J. walked back into the little office at the police station. We watched him get his phone book out and start looking.

Finally, he started dialing numbers.

Suddenly, we saw his lips moving. We couldn't hear what he was saying.

After a few minutes, he walked back into the room. He took off his glasses and cleaned them on his shirt tail.

"Your boss man is on the way," he said.

"I'11 be surprised if you boys have a job this time tomorrow. He's pretty mad."

If you want to know the truth, we really didn't care that T.J. had called Mr. Derryberry. What could he do, fire us?

We weren't thinking in those terms at the time. It just wasn't that big of a deal.

However, that was about to change.

We waited on Mr. Derryberry. We waited some more. We waited longer.

Soon, it became obvious that he wasn't coming tonight. I looked over at Mule.

He was asleep in a chair. Runt had wandered over to a corner of the room and passed out. The throbbing pain in my head was ruthless. There was no way I could sleep. I stayed up all night.

The sun finally started peeking through at 6:37 a.m. I remember looking at the clock in the police station. T.J. Middlebrooks was asleep in his chair. I could have woken Mule and Runt to make a run for it, but I didn't.

I looked out the window. Slowly but surely, a white Ford pickup truck drove up and parked in front of the building.

Mr. Derryberry had finally arrived, and he was ready to go to work.

# CHAPTER ELEVEN

Not a word was said on the way out of town. We drove almost fifty miles. That day, Clinton Derryberry was a man of few words. All three of us knew he was disappointed in our behavior. Of course, Runt and Mule sat in the backseat of the truck. I had to sit up front with Mr. Derryberry.

We didn't know where we were going.

We just knew that we were going to have to work all day long. All three of us were sick as dogs. Twice, Mr. Derryberry had to pull over for Runt to puke, and I had a splitting headache. Mule never said a word. It seemed that he was fine.

Finally, we stopped at an oil rig. By then, the temperature had risen to about 90 degrees. It eventually would make it to 100.

Mr. Derryberry surprised us after he stopped the truck. His wife had prepared sandwiches and packed potato chips and fruit. There was also plenty of water. It was all hidden in an ice chest in the back of the pickup. She knew we had to eat.

I forced myself to choke down a sandwich. Mr. Derryberry insisted that we all drink three large foam cups full of water before we started. We did as he said.

When all of that was done, Mr. Derryberry reached over into the back of his truck. He slowly pulled out three sets of manual post hole diggers. As soon as Runt saw that, he threw up again.

All day long, we dug post holes. Every now and then we got a break and pulled barbed wire. I would have worked two extra days pulling wire if I didn't have to dig post holes. Every time I stabbed the ground with the tool, my body shook and my head erupted in pain.

Runt could barely move, and I wasn't much better. Mule worked like he was sober. That was odd to me, because I was almost sure that he drank as much as me and Runt put together.

We stopped at lunch, and Mr. Derryberry let us fall asleep for about twenty minutes. I think that he knew when we woke up, we would feel even worse. He was right. I literally thought I was gonna die.

As the day went on, we did start to feel human again, and we got a system going. Mule was knocking out a pace of about ten to fifteen holes an hour.

I came in behind him and placed the poles. After that I tamped them down tight. Mr. Derryberry finally gave up on Runt digging and just made him run the three strands of wire. That was a good idea, because it kept things in order.

We were out there all day long. When dusk started setting, all four of us set the wire to the posts. When we were finished, man had never seen a prettier fence.

On the way home, Runt slept like a dead cow. Mule sat in the back seat and never said a word. I sat up front and talked to Mr. Derryberry.

"Kid," he started the conversation, "that was some pretty good fence building out there today, wasn't it?" I smiled at him. "Yes Sir," I answered.

"We really got it going there for a while, didn't we?"

A few minutes passed before Mr.

Derryberry spoke again. "Kid," he said, "I'm gonna change the course."

"What do you mean?" I asked.

"We're gonna focus on the fence business," he answered. "We got something going here. There is a strong demand for fencing around here." I have to admit that what he said didn't register with me. I was still pretty hung over.

"Yeah," Mr. Derryberry continued, "we're gonna focus on one thing for a while, building fences. We can be the best fence builders in the country, don't you think?"

Suddenly, it hit me. Mule was great at digging post holes. I was pretty good at placing the posts and tamping them into the ground. Runt would end up being good at something, and Mr. Derryberry had the know-how.

We dropped Runt off at his house first.

He opened the door and headed inside.

He never said a word. Mr. Derryberry got out of the truck and spoke to Runt's mom for a while.

After that, we went to Mule's house.

Again, Mr. Derryberry went out of his way to talk to Mule's mother. I didn't pay much attention to what they were talking about. I didn't care.

After we left Mule's house, it was just me and Mr. Derryberry in the truck as we drove to my house.

A few minutes later, Mr. Derryberry started talking.

"Kid," he said, "I've made a lot of mistakes in my life." He tipped his straw hat upward and rubbed his forehead.

"Things could have been worse last night I guess, but it was pretty bad." We drove on for a while. Mr. Derryberry didn't seem to know what he wanted to say. Finally, we got to my house. My mom was sitting on the front porch waiting for us. It was dark.

When we saw her, it seemed that Mr. Derryberry gathered up some courage.

"Kid," he said, "what I want to say is that I'm still proud of you boys. Doesn't matter to me what anybody else thinks.

I think you are fine young men."

That was all he had to say. We got out of the truck and walked towards my mother. She didn't say anything either.

I stayed close to Mr. Derryberry. The three of us stood on the front porch and just looked at each other.

That was when Mr. Derryberry took his wallet out of the back pocket of his pants. He pulled out a $100 bill. It was the first time in my life that I had ever seen one. But he didn't give it to me. He gave it to my mother.

# CHAPTER TWELVE

It turned out that Clinton Derryberry was quite a complex man. The three of us knew that, because we had to listen to his stories all the time. He loved to talk, and he expected us to listen. If one of us interrupted with a question, the conversation would take off in some crazy direction about his childhood.

It was obvious that he wanted to vent about that.

Mr. Derryberry grew up as an only child on a farm about ten miles from Dodge City. His daddy, John, wasn't much for fun. Young Clinton never got to play ball, roam the streets or hang out in pool halls like us. He worked, and he worked hard.

Clinton's mother stayed in the house most of the time. She cooked, cleaned and took care of the homeplace. John made all the family decisions. That was the way it was done back in the day. She didn't make any waves with John about it, either. She pretty much did what she was told to do. Mr. Derryberry said many times that "there is nobody more pigheaded than an old farmer." He was referring to his dad and also to himself.

He often apologized to us in advance for his know- it-all-ness.

As the years went by, Mr. Derryberry told us that he started to rebel against his daddy. That would have been easy to predict. John never paid him a red cent, and that got under young Clinton's saddle to say the least. Soon, he realized that his daddy had his life planned out for him. That plan was to work for the family on the farm for the rest of his life.

He always seemed to catch our attention when he started talking about picking cotton. It was quite an education.

"You see," he would start, "there is a difference between picking cotton and pulling cotton. If you are pulling cotton, all you have to do is grab the boll right off the stalk. It's still hard work, but it doesn't butcher your hands all up." He would then make a funny claw grip with his hand that looked all spooky.

"But if you're picking cotton," he continued, "well, that means you have to get down on your knees and pick it out of the boll. Man, that's hard work! It just tears your hands to pieces, because you can't really use thick gloves. If you do, you can't get the cotton out of the boll."

Suddenly, Mr. Derryberry went from the present tense to the past tense. "We always started off picking, because my Pa never liked leaving any cotton in the field."

It seemed like he always paused at this point in the story and got sad.

"But," he continued, "we always ended up pulling it. It just took too dang long to pick it. Now they have cotton strippers," he said. "The hardest part of that is getting the gosh darn parts of the stripper on the tractor. Now, hoeing cotton," he continued, "that's another story."

Runt couldn't help himself. He had to interrupt. He couldn't take it anymore.

"Mr. Derryberry," he asked. "Did the slaves have to pick or pull the cotton?" Mr. Derryberry tipped his hat back a little on his head and scratched his nose.

"Well," he answered. "I reckon they picked it."

You could tell that he had never thought about that before.

That led to a lesson for us about the invention of the cotton gin. Mr. Derryberry usually lost our attention when he talked about that.

"Dang!" Runt interrupted him at that point. "Those slaves didn't get paid either, did they? That ain't fair!" Mr. Derryberry looked back at Runt before he answered.

"No, Runt," he said. "That sure ain't fair."

I could tell from the look on Mr. Derryberry's face that Runt's question and his own answer kind of got to him a little bit. Mr. Derryberry was a warm-hearted man, and warm-hearted men usually are good men. Runt's question prompted a bit of a speech.

"Look boys," Mr. Derryberry said to us.

"I don't want you to be like me."

He started shaking his head after he said that.

"No, I don't mean it like that. I mean, I want you to have a better view of things than me. When I was growing up, it was all work. I learned some things, but I didn't have any fun. I want you boys to have fun. I want you to have the right kind of fun, though. I don't want you to get hurt or get in trouble."

Runt and Mule were half asleep, but I was paying attention. I didn't know exactly what he meant, but I knew it was important.

"What I mean," he continued. "What I want... "

He seemed to stumble trying to get the words out of his mouth.

"What I mean is that I care about you boys. I care a lot. It means a lot to me that you work with me."

He reached into his pocket and pulled out a paper towel. There were tears in his eyes. He tried his best to drive the truck and still blow his nose, but we weaved a little bit.

The next thing you know, Mr. Derryberry was crying. It wasn't a boo hoo cry. I just noticed the tears in his eyes. He took the paper towel and rubbed the tears out. It was pretty gross watching that. After all, he had just blown his nose into that same paper towel.

"I've got a little bit of money but not enough," Mr. Derryberry continued.

"I think if we're smart, we can get this fence business going. That way we can all make some money. You boys can maybe go to college. I keep hearing about these oil field people needing fences. That's where we can really make some hay, but we have to build good fences."

At the time, I didn't know anything about a business model, but Mr. Derryberry told me all about it.

"You boys are the key," he said. "I can go out and hire older men, but it will only help me. If you boys learn this business, it will help you, too."

Things got quiet for a while. Runt and Mule had already lost interest in what Mr. Derryberry was saying. I hated it when it got quiet and there was no conversation, so I kept the talk a going.

"I've never thought about going to college," I remember saying. "I don't know if I'm smart enough." Mr. Derryberry laughed.

"Oh, you're smart enough," he answered. "You're a lot smarter than you think you are, Kid."

Things got quiet again. It seemed to me that Mr. Derryberry was getting a little uncomfortable. He looked over his shoulder into the back seat. He saw Mule snoring.

"Mule," he said a little loudly. "You ever thought about college?"

We both thought Mule was asleep, but the oddest thing happened. Suddenly, he opened his eyes and was wide awake.

"I'm going to be a banker," he said. "I wanna be rich."

That caught both me and Mr. Derryberry by surprise.

"That's great, Mule," Mr. Derryberry said. "But you need to know that the banker usually isn't the guy who is rich.

The guy who puts the money in the bank is the guy who is rich."

Mule wasn't intimidated at all.

"I know that," he said, "but I've got to start somewhere."

"Well, I'm impressed," Mr. Derryberry answered. "I want to get rich, too. I hope we can do it together." He twisted his back in a funny way so he could get a look at the other character in the back seat.

"What about you Runt? Have you ever thought about going to college?" he asked.

Runt stretched out his arms, and then he rubbed his eyes.

"I'm gonna hit it big in the oil business," he answered. "I'm gonna do it by building fences." We all laughed.

Mr. Derryberry drove on down the road. It got quiet again. After a while, he started telling some story about harvesting wheat, and there was no need for me to carry the conversation. I started thinking. Nobody, including Mr. Derryberry, asked me about going to college. Nobody asked me how I was gonna make my fortune. I guess they just took it for granted that I was along for the same ride as them.

# CHAPTER THIRTEEN

Slowly, Derryberry fencing started to grow. The oil boom wasn't nearly as exciting and profitable when you were directly involved in it. "The glamour wears off fast," Mr. Derryberry used to say. The truth was that there wasn't that much of an oil boom going on at all.

Runt, Mule and I were more interested in sports, girls and hanging out at the pool hall, not necessarily in that order, than working. However, Mr. Derryberry was focused on business. Almost every Saturday was fence building day. He believed in making it as fun as possible.

Mrs. Derryberry planned the breakfast and lunch menu for us all week. We ate better on workdays than any other day of the week. Then one Saturday, things changed forever.

It was early March of our senior year in high school. The weather that day was typical of early spring on the high plains. Cold, blustery winds tore right through our clothes. Nobody wanted to work that day. Mule had been sick all week. I remember pulling up to his house early that morning. We didn't even have to knock. He was waiting for us. When he opened the door and got into the back seat of the truck, he started hacking, sneezing and carrying on like he had pneumonia. I remember how sharp his cough sounded. It scared me.

Mr. Derryberry was adamant that he couldn't work, so he ordered him back into the house. Mule argued for a little bit, but he knew he had no business being out in the field that day. He got out of the truck and went back to his house. I'll never forget the look he gave us before walking in the front door. It was like he knew something was wrong.

Mr. Derryberry, Runt and I drove about twenty miles to the worksite. It was an old run-down farm. Mr. Derryberry told us on the way that somebody had just bought the farm and wanted to put up new fencing. He didn't tell us who.

Our job that day was to start building a simple barb-wire fence around 20 acres of pasture. Later, we would build a fence all the way around the entire quarter section of land.

You could tell how excited Mr. Derryberry was to be there. It was his biggest contract to date, and he wanted to do a great job.

We started off slow, because it was just so darn cold. Runt wasn't into it, and neither was I. However, I knew someone was going to have to coax Runt into working, so I tried my best.

I decided to get him talking about his favorite subject, baseball.

Runt was really a good player. He excelled as a shortstop on the school and summer league teams. A junior college team wanted him to come to school and play for them. He was tall and rangy with a strong arm. Not only could he hit for average but he could also hit with power. He was really fast, too. Everybody knew he had a future in the sport. He was also a good football player, but he didn't have the love for the game like he did baseball.

Mule, on the other hand, was a lineman on the football team. He was a pretty good player, too. However, he was under six foot tall and his footwork was only average.

I only played football and baseball because of Runt and Mule. I wanted to be with them. I was never any count at either. I mainly warmed the bench.

I got the conversation going. "Who was the best hitter of all time, Runt?"

Runt seemed disinterested at first, but with some prodding he perked up a little.

We were right behind the water tank working on punching out holes for the corner post section of the fence.

Of course, that was usually Mule's job.

Runt stabbed his post hole digger into the ground and took off his gloves.

Though it was cold, he was starting to break a little bit of a sweat.

"I would have to go with Pete Rose," he said confidently. "He's gonna break the all-time hit record, you know."

The fact was that I didn't know, but I didn't let on about it. Runt kept talking.

"Yeah," he said, "he plays for The Big Red Machine, the Cincinnati Reds. I love to watch them play on TV." I could sense that Mr. Derryberry was watching us from a distance. He was working on getting the other materials ready. I knew my job, and that was to get some work out of Runt today. But it was harder than I thought it would be to do. We couldn't get the holes dug and cleaned out like we needed. If Mule would have been there, it would have been no problem. He was so strong and good with post hole diggers. It was amazing! However, neither myself nor Runt were very good at it at all.

We dug, and we dug, and we dug.

Finally, we attempted to set the poles.

Mr. Derryberry had a perplexed look on his face. He knew we hadn't done a very good job, but it was really cold.

We couldn't move on until we set the corner post.

Finally, Mr. Derryberry decided to set the post. We set the corner post and attached onto two other posts to form a V at the property line. When we were finished, the corner posts didn't look straight. The job looked pretty bad.

Mr. Derryberry stared at the corner post for five minutes.

"I think we're gonna have to dig it out and start over again," he said quietly.

It was pretty obvious that he was disappointed in us.

Just as soon as he said it, a red pickup truck came flying down the road towards us. Dirt and gravel were flying behind it. The wind was howling. It was cold and miserable.

The red pickup turned towards us and came to a quick stop. The door swung open and somebody jumped out of the truck. We had to shield our eyes from all the debris that was flying.

After a few seconds, the air cleared. I dropped my arm away from my eyes. I identified the man who got out of the red pickup. It was Tom Wayne Rhyner.

56   GERLAD BRENCE

truck. We had to shield our eyes from all the debris that was flying.

# CHAPTER FOURTEEN

Tom Wayne slammed the door so loud I thought it was going to break the windows.

"That's the worst looking corner post I've ever seen!" he screamed. "I'm not paying for that! Pull it out of the ground, and start over!"

Mr. Derryberry was pretty calm, but he was concerned.

"I know, I know," he answered. "We'll fix it, Tom Wayne. We'll fix it."

But Tom Wayne wasn't satisfied with that answer.

"Fix it right now," he yelled. "Get back to work, and get it corrected." It was almost five o'clock in the evening. There was only about an hour of sunlight left. Mr. Derryberry tried to explain.

"Tom Wayne," he said. "These boys have been out here diggin' all day long.

We'll come back in the morning and get back to work. I promise you."

Tom Wayne, however, was unimpressed.

"Well," he said, "that's not good enough. You get it done tonight. I don't care how long you've been digging.

I'm paying you good money to get this fence built."

Runt and I had kept our mouths shut up to this point, but the next comment from Tom Wayne Rhyner set us both off.

"Listen old man," Tom Wayne continued, "you get over to the truck and pick up that post hole digger yourself. I want you to do it, not this snot nosed kids!"

Runt started taking off his coat as he marched straight to Tom Wayne.

"Don't you talk to Mr. Derryberry like that!" he yelled. "I was the one who was doing the digging, and I'll be the one to fixit."

Of course, thinking back on all of this now, I know that was exactly what Tom Wayne Rhyner wanted Runt to say.

It opened the door to a major league conflict.

"Well, Boy," Tom Wayne answered, "it sure doesn't surprise me that you're responsible. I don't think you've got enough salt in your pants to get a job like that done. I told my old man not to hire you guys. What a joke!"

Runt kept his cool. He walked over to grab the post hole diggers. On the way, his shoulder glanced Tom Wayne's shoulder. Runt didn't seem to notice, but Tom Wayne did.

"Hey, you punk!" Tom Wayne yelled.

"You got a problem? Just come out and say it!"

Runt grabbed the post hole diggers and a shovel. He walked towards the corner posts. In a flash, he was digging like his life depended on it.

I grabbed a shovel myself and helped.

Mr. Derryberry did the same. The three of us worked as hard as we could work.

It was okay to me that I was humiliated, but I didn't like the fact that Tom Wayne had gone out of his way to embarrass Mr. Derryberry. I know Runt felt the same way.
It got quiet for a few minutes, then it got dark, really dark. We dug in the dark like we were digging a body out of a cemetery grave. It was demeaning to say the least.

I could feel the energy level lowering as the time ticked away. We weren't making much progress if you wanted to know the truth. We were just putting in some time to make Tom Wayne happy. I knew that approach wasn't going to last long.

You would think that Tom Wayne would have gotten cold himself. The smart thing to do would have been just to go home. We were all wasting our time, but he couldn't help himself.

He got back into his pickup truck and started the engine. I'm sure he turned on the heater. He did not shine his lights on us over at the corner posts.

We dug for another hour while Tom Wayne sat in the pickup. Finally, Mr. Derryberry spoke.

"That's it boys," he said. "We're going home!"

He said it with a lot of confidence.

Mr. Derryberry walked over to his truck, and he started the engine.

Suddenly, the headlights flashed. Before Runt and I knew it, he was throwing the post hole diggers, shovels and any other tool we were using into the back of the truck. We started helping him.

Suddenly, Tom Wayne jumped out of his truck.

"What are you doing?" he screamed at us. "You're not finished with the job!" He was carrying a big lantern in his right hand.

"We're out of here," Mr. Derryberry responded.

"No, you're not!" shouted Tom Wayne.

"You're gonna finish the job tonight!"

Mr. Derryberry starred a hole through him.

"You can wait 'til tomorrow, or you can fire us," he shouted. "But I'm taking these boys home!"

Mr. Derryberry continued to load the truck. However, Tom Wayne was stubborn as an old goat. By then, Runt and I were pretty much just spectators.

"Get back out here and finish the job, Old Man!" Tom Wayne screamed.

However, it did no good. Mr. Derryberry had made up his mind.

Tom Wayne went into a rage. He ran over to Mr. Derryberry and grabbed him with his left hand. He yanked his coat pretty hard, and Mr. Derryberry stumbled backwards.

Before I knew it, Runt was right at the scene. He threw a roundhouse punch at Tom Wayne, but he didn't connect. Tom Wayne retaliated. He swung the lantern straight at Runt's head. It hit him in the left eye and down he went.

I usually was pretty cowardly in these situations, but I charged Tom Wayne.

However, he knew he had really hurt Runt, so he kinda fell down easy.

Mr. Derryberry went into shock.

He couldn't move. Runt was lying helplessly on the ground. I got up and tried to help, but I didn't know what to do.

I don't really remember much after that. I drove the truck to the hospital.

Mr. Derryberry sat in the backseat attending to Runt. I don't remember what happened to Tom Wayne Rhyner.

One thing will always haunt me until the day I die. I'll always wonder what would have happened that day if Mule would have been with us.

# CHAPTER FIFTEEN

Neither runt nor mule ever questioned my plan to pull the pickup truck and the cattle trailer across the bridge with a tow rope. I wish they would have, but they didn't. They just did what I told 'em to do.

We got the towrope out of the back of the pickup and wrapped it around the front fender. Mule tied it around his waist and stretched it tight. I would say that he was about ten feet in front of the truck.

Runt volunteered to drive. I got behind the trailer and tried to keep everything balanced. I thought I had pulled one over on the both of them. There wasn't much that I could do to help solve the problem where I was positioned, and I thought the pressure was off of me.

As soon as I got set, I realized that I was gonna have to deal with the cattle.

We had thirteen of them crammed into the trailer. Even though they were just cattle, I thought it was inhumane what we were doing to them. They were mooing, screaming and drooling all over each other.

"All right, Boys!" Runt screamed from inside the truck. "Let's get this show on the road!" Slowly but surely, Mule leaned forward and started trying to walk, but we didn't go anywhere. Mule stopped to gather his strength, and Runt got all over him.

"Come on, Mule!" he yelled. "You gotta do better n' that!"

Once again, Mule leaned forward and tried to pull the truck. Once again, the cattle mooed and bellowed. Suddenly, Mule slipped and fell down. When he hit the tracks, the bridge started wobbling and shaking.

"Moooooooh!" the cattle yelled again.

They knew what was going on.

I made my way around to the front.

That was when I noticed that the truck was in first gear and the emergency brake was on. Runt didn't know to put the truck in neutral.

Mule was out on the foot of the bridge getting ready to start pulling again. I walked gingerly out to him and grabbed the towrope.

"Mule," I said, "give me a minute. The truck is still in gear."

I'll never forget the puzzled look on his face. He didn't know what that meant.

I walked back to the truck. Runt was bouncing up and down on the seat.

"Come on, Mule!" he yelled. "You can do it!"

It took me awhile to convince Runt that I needed to drive. I had come to terms that if he drove, we would end up in the river. He relented, and all three of us got back into position. Mule was out front with the rope. I was driving, and Runt was now behind the trailer.

By now, the cattle were really restless.

They started stomping their hooves and banging on the walls. It was hard to focus on anything with all the noise they were making.

"Mule," I yelled, "wait til I say "go" before you take off. Let me get everything steady."

I waited for everything to calm down.

Runt was behind the trailer pouting, but he put his shoulder down and was ready to push.

I gathered up all the courage I could muster and released the emergency brake. Next, I put the truck in neutral.

"Go Mule, start pulling!" I yelled it as loud as I could.

Mule leaned forward and gave it his all.

The truck started to move. The cattle started to moo and scream again.

We seemed to be going pretty good for about twenty feet or so when Runt started screaming in the back.

"Stop! Stop! Stop!" he yelled.

I hit the brakes. When I did that, it jerked Mule straight back towards the truck. He hit the tracks of the bridge with a thud.

The bridge was swinging sideways now. The cattle were going crazy, but Runt was hollering so loud that he almost drowned them out. By the time I got out of the truck and made it to the back of the trailer, Mule was already there. He was bent over howling.

As soon as I saw what he saw, I started laughing myself. One of those cows had puked right out of the back of that trailer, and it all landed right on top of Runt's head. I have to say that it was the funniest thing I've ever seen in my life!

# CHAPTER SIXTEEN

Going to college was an adventure for all three of us. Mule had an uncle who attended junior college for a year. Runt's aunt tried to make it at Wichita State but failed. Me, I never had anybody in my family who ever even attempted higher education.

However, Mr. Derryberry insisted that all three of us at least consider it.

He pushed us about it constantly. He said we could work for him during the summer and holiday breaks to help pay for it.

We started out at the local Junior College. Mule liked college the most.

His grades were adequate but not great.

I held my own, but I was no honor student. Runt barely got by. He spent most of his time in the student union hustling pool games.

Runt really wanted to play baseball.

However, after Tom Wayne Rhyner knocked out his left eye with a lantern, it really wasn't possible. There was no way he could hit college pitching.

Struggling through life with a glass eye and false teeth was pretty difficult when you are only approaching twenty years old. Mule and I did what we could do to keep his spirits high, but it was tough. Sometimes, Runt would go into a funk that was just terrible. I think not being able to play baseball hurt him the most.

However, Runt always found a way to have fun. One cold afternoon during Christmas vacation we were all at Mule's place watching TV. There was nothing to do and nowhere to go. It was snowing sideways outside, and only a fool would go out in the weather.

Mule and I didn't notice so much that Runt had disappeared. We were watching Gilligan's Island. Suddenly, he appeared out of a bedroom.

He almost scared us to death as he stumbled out the door and walked like he was a cripple across the room. He had taken his glass eye out of the socket.

It was easy to see the red, gooey backlog where his eye was supposed to be. I turned my head to hide.

The show didn't stop there. Suddenly, Runt smiled. He had taken his false teeth out, too! It looked horrible! Runt got right up in Mule's personal space and torqued his face to look even scarier. Mule almost punched him out.

That would have just made Runt uglier, though.

He made a couple of rounds around the room with his arms out like he was an airplane. Mule's sister, Twyla, came out of her room to see what the commotion was all about.

Runt did everything in his power to scare her, but she wouldn't give in to his immature tactics. "You are so childish, Runt!" she all but yelled. "You should be ashamed of yourself!"

After a couple more laps around the living room, Runt slipped back into the bathroom. A few seconds passed, then Mule, Twyla and I all started laughing.

"What was that?" Mule asked.

Runt could have worked in a carnival freak show and made a fortune.

Five minutes later, he walked back into the room like nothing happened. He sat down in a chair and commenced to watching TV. It was Twyla who asked the first question.

"Runt," she asked, "do you make a habit of doing that?"

Runt gave his pat response. "Do what?" he answered.

"You know what," Twyla responded.

"Do you take your eye and your teeth out around people very often?"

"I don't know what you are talking about," he answered. "Is there anything else on TV besides these jokers?"

We all sat there for a while saying nothing. It did occur to me that Runt scared me so bad I didn't even really remember what he looked like without his eye and his teeth. I kinda wanted to see it again.

Mule sat over in the corner. He was still laughing.

"Really, Runt," he said, "do you do that very often?"

I realized that I had never seen him do it before, and I was around him almost every day. How come this hadn't come up before?

Runt just sat there and watched TV. He acted like nothing had happened and would not join the conversation about his appearance.

A couple of hours later it was time to go home. I was driving my old beat-up truck. I jumped in the driver's seat. Runt stepped into the passenger door.

On the way home, we started talking about school and other things. Finally, I pulled up to his house. Before he got out of the truck, I had to say something about the missing teeth and eye thing.

"Runt," I asked, "what the heck was that all about? It scared the dog out of us."

Runt looked straight out the front windshield, but he did answer my question before he got out of the pickup.

"It was a test," he answered. "I just wanted to see how you guys would react."

I didn't know what to say. I could tell for a moment that he wanted a little feedback from me, so I gave it to him.

"It was awful," I said, "but I kinda enjoyed it."

"Well," he said before he closed the door. "You don't want to get used to it."

# CHAPTER SEVENTEEN

As we got older, it seemed that Mr. Derryberry's business started to fizzle. He was getting older, and Mule, Runt and I were interested in other things. Making more money was one of them.

Mule and Runt bounced from odd job to odd job, but I pretty much just stayed with Mr. Derryberry. Every now and then, one of us would come across something pretty good. By now, we had invested quite a bit of time and money into junior college. It was time to figure out if we should stay in school or go to work.

Mule had a natural reputation as a tough guy. Nobody seemed to want to mess with him. He wasn't that tall, but he was stocky and strong, very strong.

One thing led to another, and he landed a job as a night watchman for the Pinkerton Security Company.

His job was to guard the local pharmacy. He sat in his car all night in front of the store. The job paid well, and it wasn't hard. However, it gets cold in Kansas during the winter. On top of that, staying awake all night and dealing with the boredom was tough.

Of course, Runt and I knew exactly where the pharmacy was and what time Mule went to work. We thought we had grown out of our immature hijinks and practical jokes by then. However, Mule wasn't so sure about that. Every night, he expected us to tool him around.

He decided to make a plan. If either of us tried to scare him, trick him or embarrass him, it would be a big mistake. He had some ideas. Every night, he watched for us. It helped him stay awake and alert.

Mule didn't carry a gun while he worked for the Pinkertons. He was just under 21 years old, so it wouldn't be legal anyway. At that point in our lives, none of us ever had much to do with guns.

The only weapon Mule had was a big flashlight. He was supposed to get out of his old car, a '69 Oldsmobile Cutlass Supreme, and walk around the pharmacy every hour.

One night, Mule was walking around the pharmacy at about two a.m. It was a really windy night. All of a sudden, a big black bird came swooping down. It scared the heck out of him. At first, he thought it was one of us.

The bird flew by Mule's head then turned around and came back. Mule ducked on the first flyby, but he didn't duck on the second. The bird came back in on him and met his death when Mule clubbed him with the flashlight.

A couple of months later, a coyote came milling through town. Mule was doing his hourly walk when he came face to face with the varmint in the alley.

The coyote growled at Mule. Mule growled back at the coyote. Suddenly, the coyote turned hide tail and ran away.

Then one evening we just couldn't help ourselves. It was a Saturday night, and Runt was up to no good. By then, Mule was used to the steady pay. He wouldn't take a night off from guarding the pharmacy for anything.

Runt and I missed hanging out with him. At a little before one in the morning, Runt drove to the pharmacy. I just happened to be in the car with him.

We parked a few blocks away to think about what we were gonna do. We decided to go back to our old tactics. We would throw rocks at him.

To the pharmacy we went, carrying about five rocks each. It was a warm night, so there weren't any distractions.

There was a full moon. Though it was the middle of the night, visibility was good.

We hid behind the library steps across the street. We could see Mule's old car, but it was too dark to see if he was inside. Runt started snickering.

"We're gonna scare the crap out of him!" He was very confident when he said it.

Runt fired the first rock. It hit the wall of the pharmacy. I threw the next one.

It was a misfire and bounced off the ground into the front window. I didn't want to do that. There was never any intention to cause any damage. We just wanted to mess with Mule and have some fun. Runt fired another harmless rock at his car.

However, our mood was about to change. Out of the blue, a rock came flying directly towards us. It blasted the guard rail two feet away from our heads. A couple of seconds later, another rock crashed into the steps just in front of us. A third rock hit Runt in the shoulder. Another rock whizzed by my head.

"Let's get out of here!" Runt yelled.

It didn't take long for me to agree. We squirmed, crawled and scurried to the back of the library and took off running.

As we turned the corner and headed towards Runt's old pickup, another barrage of rocks came flying towards us. Most of them either flew over our heads or hit the street in front of us. It felt like we were the target of machine gun fire.

We got to the truck and jumped in the cab. We were still keeping our heads down out of fear. Runt fired up the ignition and put it in gear. There was really only one way to go. That was back towards the pharmacy.

Runt stepped on the gas, and we flew down the road. When we got to the library neither of us could help but to look across the street. They're stood Mule Archer. He was holding a bucket in his left hand and a rock in his right.

# CHAPTER EIGHTEEN

Life was moving fast. I started commuting to Kansas University and did okay. I figured I would major in business. After that, I would help Mr. Derryberry with his business.

Unfortunately, Runt never did well in school. He was too busy hustling pool and hanging out at the student union.

After he quit junior college, he bounced around from odd job to odd job.

However, Mule was focused. He really liked his job as a nightwatchman and wanted to move forward into police work. Kansas had a pretty good program for students who were interested in criminal justice.

He kept his job as the nightwatchman at the pharmacy. Steady work was hard to find for college kids, and he was very reliable. Often on weekend nights, Runt and I would go down to the pharmacy.

We would hang out with him while he worked. Of course, we always made sure to tell him that we were coming.

One night we were talking about the future. "I don't know what I need to do," Runt said. "I don't know if I'll make it as a professional pool player."

"I think I'm gonna be a police officer,"

Mule added. "I like it, and I think I'm pretty good at it."

Mule was always a man of few words, and his confidence impressed me.

Neither Runt nor Mule seemed to be interested in what I was going to do, so I didn't say anything. To our surprise, Mule kept talking.

"There aren't very many bad guys around here," he said. "This is a boring job. It's all I can do to keep my sanity. It gets pretty lonely in the middle of the night."

"Well, you could be building fence like me and Runt," I said. "We wouldn't have to dig all those post holes by ourselves if you were around."

Mule laughed. "Don't you guys have any schooling?" he asked. "You need to get you a nice, safe job like me. To heck with that manual labor!"

Runt and I did make eye contact for a second. We both realized that he was right. The conversation turned serious when Runt told us that he had a girlfriend. That was new. Up until that point, it was just the three of us. There was never any interference by any woman.

She had just moved into town from Cooperton, Oklahoma. Neither myself nor Mule was impressed that Runt was dating a girl from Oklahoma.

Runt commenced to telling us all about her. She was very committed to school, and he thought that he was in love with her. He also added that she came from a wealthy family.

"A girlfriend?" Mule asked. "You ain't even got a steady job, Runt! You don't have no business having a girlfriend." I kept my mouth shut. I could tell that Runt was already peeved at Mule's comments.

"Well, I've got to make something out of myself, then," Runt answered. His pride was on the line now.

"I love this girl. You guys wouldn't understand. No girl wants anything to do with either one of you."

Mule smiled. "I hope you know what you're doing," he added. "Be careful getting attached, Runt. You might be in a little over your head. You ain't even got any teeth, and you only have one eye. Does she know that?"

"I ain't in over my head," Runt responded. "I wish I hadn't even told you about her."

You could tell that his feelings were hurt.

"She doesn't know about my teeth or my eye," he responded. "I was hoping that you might be able to help me figure out a way to tell her, but you have to be all negative."

Things got quiet for a while. I didn't know what to say. I could tell that Runt was mad, but Mule was upset, too. I sensed that he was jealous.

Finally, Mule responded. "Well," he said. "I'll have to think about that for a while."

# CHAPTER NINETEEN

A couple of months went by after that conversation. Mule went to school during the morning. He would take care of whatever business he needed to take care of after lunch. After that, he would grab a few hours of sleep before getting ready for his watchman shift at dusk.

It was a very boring, lonely existence, but he didn't seem to mind. One night in late February, he followed his normal routine. He had eaten a bigger than normal meal that evening, and he felt sluggish. The time dragged on and on.

He was bored more than usual and around 11:00, he fell asleep.

His car was parked to the right of the front door about thirty yards away.

Suddenly, his eyes popped open, and he awoke. He looked at his watch. It was almost midnight. He realized that he needed to get out of the car and make a trip around the pharmacy. That's exactly what he did.

It was pitch dark. The skies were cloudy, so there was no light from the moon. It was windy and cold.

Mule pulled his coat tight. He made a left turn around to the alley. All was good. He walked the back side of the pharmacy which faced a large parking lot. All was good. He turned left again around the side of the pharmacy that faced the old library. All was good. Then he turned the corner and walked up to the front door.

Mule Archer was one of those guys that could sense trouble and ramp up the intensity like fire burning down a wick. Something wasn't right. The door was ajar as he approached it.

When he got to the door, he thought about flipping on the flashlight, but he decided not to do it. He looked to his left and then to his right. He turned around to look across the street. Everything seemed in order.

"Runt!" he screamed half-heartedly. "Is that you?"

There was no answer. The wind howled eerily. Mule tried to gain control of his hair.

"Kid, is that you in there?" he whispered loudly. "I swear you guys' better knock it off. This isn't funny!" Again, there was no answer. All was quiet. The only sound was the wind blowing.

"They forgot to lock the front door," he thought to himself.

"If you guys are in this store, there's gonna be a serious whoopin'!" He yelled it this time. "I'm coming in there!" He slowly opened the door. He was expecting me and Runt to try to scare him out of his underwear. He smiled as he walked in the door, because he was sure we were in the building.

It was dark, really dark inside the pharmacy. Mule flipped on the big flashlight. A stream of light shot out like a laser.

He started walking slowly through the first aisle of the store. Suddenly, he banged into a shelf full of band aids.

They fell to the floor. Mule dropped to a knee and started picking them up.

When he finished, he stood up. He was not supposed to be inside the store. Of course, he knew that. The thought hit him that all three of us would be in big trouble if we didn't get out of there, now.

"Runt! Kid!" he yelled. "I'll get fired if we don't get out of here. Now come on. This ain't funny!" There was no answer.

Mule turned left and started slowly walking around the corner. It was time to walk down the next aisle. He was careful not to knock anything else off the shelves. Everything was quiet.

He turned the next corner to his right and started walking down the third aisle.

"Any second now," he thought, "either Runt or Kid is gonna jump up and try to scare me."

But neither of us showed. He came to the end of the aisle and turned left.

There was only one more aisle left. He was at the back of the store. That was where the pharmacy was located. That was where the drugs were. It was a store locked up inside a bigger store. The band aids, mouthwash, and vitamins were really just a side business.

Mule peered in at the pharmacy.

"Those knuckleheads wouldn't hide in there, would they?" he thought to himself.

You could have heard a snake slither it was so quiet. Mule walked over to the pharmacy door and turned the handle.

To his surprise, it was unlocked.

He opened the door. As soon as he did, someone flew by him at ground level.

He turned quickly. Suddenly, a second person did the same.

"I'm gonna kill you guys!" Mule shouted. He was laughing as he said it.

Mule was always smart. Instead of following them, he took off the other way. That was to his left. He would cut them off at the door. Around the aisle he went to the front of the store.

When he got there, he knew he had to do something quick or they would get away. He turned into their lane. There was a collision. The wreck blasted him right into both intruders. Mule looked at his victims. The first thought that went through his mind was, "That's not Runt and Kid!"

The fight was on. It doesn't matter how big and strong you are, two against one is a tough battle. Mule slugged one thief, then he tackled the other. The one he slugged got up and ran for the door.

Mule got up and tackled him.

The second thief tried to get away, but Mule reached up and grabbed him by the ankle with his left hand. He held the first thief down with his right arm. The battle continued. Suddenly, one of the thieves got out the door. Mule picked up the other thief and started chasing the one who got away.

Most people don't believe this next part, but Mule swears it happened.

That's why I believe him. He carried one of the crooks around the waist while he ran down the other one. That was when the real whoopin' started!

When the beating was over, Mule dragged both of them back to the pharmacy. He took them inside and planted them against the wall. It was time to call the police. At that point, neither of the two crooks would dare try to take on Mule Archer again.

The police arrived, and Mule told them the whole story. It turned out that those guys had robbed several pharmacies in Eastern Kansas. The law had been trying to catch them for months.

Mule started putting everything back into place. It took him a couple of hours.

He knew that people who worked at the pharmacy would start arriving at 6:30 a.m. It was then that he realized that he nor the local police had thought about calling the store owner.

When he was finished, Mule left the store exactly the way it was when they closed the doors the night before. Back to his car he went. Soon people started showing up to work. When they did, Mule did the same thing he did every morning. He started his car and drove away.

He liked to stop at a donut shop on his way home. As he got out of the car, he sensed something odd. He noticed that people were staring at him. It felt unnatural. But you know, word travels fast in a small town. He didn't realize that a legend had just been born.

# CHAPTER TWENTY

Mule's heroics were the talk of the town. The fascination of what he did astonished everyone.

Of course, he wanted to hear none of it.

He just wanted to go about his business.

He had some momentum going in school, and he had always liked his night watchman job.

People started stopping him on the streets and asking him about the attempted robbery. As you might expect, there was some exaggeration.

Before you knew it, the story was that Mule had dodged gunfire. He was always the first one to correct that tale.

Soon, a news reporter from Kansas City showed up at his house. Twyla met him at the door. She was excited about the attention her brother was receiving, and she told the reporter all about what happened. Mule was asleep and had given her orders that he not to be bothered.

"Yeah," Twyla started, "Mule has always been stronger than most other people. It's just natural. It didn't surprise me when I heard about what he did to those crooks!"

The reporter sucked up everything she said and wrote it in his notebook. That weekend, Mule's picture was on the front page of the Kansas City Monitor.

The news story was accurate, but the headline was worrisome. The article labeled Mule as The Midnight Rider, because the incident at the pharmacy happened right around twelve o'clock at night. Later the story warned bad guys, not to mess with this Mule!

After a few days, things started to get back to normal. Runt, Mule and I hung out at the pool hall and drank beer together when we had some time off from our affairs.

One night, Mule started talking. That was uncharacteristic of him.

"You just think you want to be famous," he said. "I don't like it. I wish all this stuff had never happened."

Runt didn't cut him any slack.

"Come on, Mule," he said. "You're the town hero. I don't know why you are even hanging out with a couple of do-nothing guys like me and Kid." You could tell that Mule took offense to that.

"Don't ever say that again, Runt!" He said it with authority. "I just want things to be the way they used to be. I ain't no big shot."

Runt wouldn't shut up, though. He kept talking while we were playing pool and drinking beer. It was early in the evening on a Saturday night. Suddenly, the door opened and in walked Mr. Derryberry He had never been in the pool hall before. Immediately, he took off his hat and walked over to us. We all noticed that he was carrying the newspaper article about Mule from the Kansas City Monitor.

"Hello fellas," he said. "I was just wondering if we could visit for a while?"

Mule and Runt had drifted away from Mr. Derryberry, but I had not. He had fallen on some hard times and his health was deteriorating.

"Can we sit over there at that table and visit?" he asked.

Of course, we did as he said. All three of us put away our beer before we sat down. It would have been disrespectful to Mr. Derryberry to drink in front of him.

He scratched his head before he spoke.

Finally, he was ready.

"Boys," he started. "I'm really proud of the three of ya."

Mule and Runt noticed how frail and gaunt that he looked. They were a little shocked. Mr. Derryberry had always had a robust appearance.

"You are all gonna do good things," he added, "but there is something that I think I need to tell you." He looked all three of us directly in the eye, one at a time. "I've never told you that I was a state trooper back in the old days. I enjoyed my time there, but I had some trouble."

He seemed to slouch down in his chair a little like he was sick. We didn't know what to think.

"I'm concerned about this newspaper article, Mule," he said. "It's not that I'm not proud for you. It's just that I know where this might lead."

Mule looked straight at me. I could tell what he was thinking. He was wondering what this was all about.

Mr. Derryberry continued. "I've seen this before. You see, when you get in the papers for something like this, it angers some people. They might challenge you."

That statement got our attention.

Runt chimed into the conversation.

"What do you mean, challenge him?"

Runt's reaction startled me a little.

Mule sat over in the corner with no expression on his face.

Mr. Derryberry stared at Mule.

"You better be careful, Mule." He said it with conviction. "You already have quite a reputation. It doesn't matter that you are just a night watchman.

They'll consider you a law man."

Mule was already worried that what Mr. Derryberry was trying to say was true. It helped to hear the reinforcement.

"We better get you a gun," Mr. Derryberry said softly.

"I'm serious, Son."

It got really quiet in a place that was usually really loud. Suddenly, the front door swung open. A whole crew of guys entered the building. Before we knew it, Tom Wayne Rhyner was standing right in front of us.

# CHAPTER TWENTY - ONE

Tom Wayne's entrance into the pool hall made me realize why the great gunfighters of the West always sat with their backs to the wall. Mule was sitting at the table with his back to the door. If Tom Wayne would have come in there with a weapon, he could have easily taken Mule out. That didn't happen, but there was a lesson to be learned.

We all stood up when we saw Tom Wayne, and we expected trouble. Tom Wayne slowly walked around us. When he got about five feet away, he stopped.

"Well boys," he said smugly, "if it ain't the bona fide hero of the town, Mule Archer!"

He started laughing.

"You know Mule," he continued.

"When I heard about your exploits I wondered if you cheap shot 'em like you did me?"

By then, it was very quiet in the pool hall.

"So, is that how you whooped them robbers, Mule? Did you sucker punch 'em like you did me?"

Mule was calm, but Runt was getting antsy. Mr. Derryberry put his right hand on his shoulder as to say, "Be quiet."

"We don't want any trouble," Mule said. "That was in the past, Tom Wayne."

Tom Wayne stepped closer to Mule.

They almost got nose to nose. Suddenly, the owner of the pool hall came over to make sure a fight wasn't gonna start.

"You boys take this outside," he all but screamed. "I can't afford you tearing the place up again."

Mule, nor Tom Wayne would budge.

They just stared at each other. The mutual hate was pretty obvious.

Finally, Tom Wayne broke the silence.

"Well, Mule," he said. "I can't pick a fight with the town hero now, can I?" He turned and walked over to the pool table. "That ain't good politics!"

He put a quarter into the slot on the side of the table and pulled the lever to release the pool balls. The loud rumbling noise of the balls banging against the inside of the table was very uncomfortable.

Tom Wayne stood upright and looked back at us.

"But your day will come, Mule. I promise."

Mule didn't hesitate. "What do you mean by that?" he asked.

Tom Wayne smiled. "I don't like you, Mule," he said. He started racking up the pool table for a game. "People I don't like usually don't have very good luck round here, did you know that?" he added.

Mule looked over at Runt who looked back at him. There was quite a bit of tension.

Mr. Derryberry decided to speak for the first time.

"Boys, I think it would be a good idea to get on out of here," he said.

However, Mule was not the kind of guy who gave in to intimidation. He sat back down in his chair.

"In all due respect, Mr. Derryberry," he said. "I think I will stay right here." Mr. Derryberry looked a little perplexed.

"Well," he said. "I have to go."

Before he left the table, he looked back at Mule one more time. "Remember what I said, Son," he said. "I'll talk to you soon."

I couldn't believe that Runt had stayed quiet that long, but he didn't know what to say.

Finally, he spoke. "I've never seen anybody so stubborn as you Mule. Let's go."

"You go on," he answered. "I'm staying for a while."

Runt couldn't believe it. "What do you think you are going to accomplish?' he asked.

Mule leaned back in his chair before he spoke. "I'll tell you what I'll accomplish," he answered. "Somebody has to stand up to bullies. Tom Wayne

Rhyner doesn't get to decide what I do and what I don't do."

Runt threw up his hands and sat back down. I went to the bar and bought three beers. I knew we were going to be there for a while.

# CHAPTER TWENTY - TWO

Soon, a new character came into our lives. Her name was Macy Hall, Runt's new girlfriend.

The romance with his first girlfriend from Oklahoma had flamed out pretty quickly. Macy was the daughter of a well-to- do businessman. Runt met her through a mutual friend, and tau changed his life forever.

Macy was a beautiful girl. She was tall with long, black hair. She tolerated me and Mule, but it was pretty obvious that she didn't care for us. We sensed that, so we just ran the option away from her when we could.

Before you knew it, Runt was a goner.

He spent almost all of his time with her.

However, there were problems from the start of their relationship. Macy was from a white-collar family. She was used to having money.

Runt was, well, blue collar at best. He was not a good student. Never finishing college was going to be a chain around his neck with her family to say the least.

They fought often, and they fought loud. Mule and I both knew their relationship was doomed, but Runt was totally head over heels in love with her.

At the ripe old age of 22, he proposed.

Macy's father objected, but that didn't matter. Macy and Runt were both hard headed, and they would defeat the world. At least they thought they would. A year later, they had their first child. They named her Georgia. At the time, Runt was working for the county.

Of course, that lifestyle didn't go over well with Macy's parents, especially her father. Macy and Runt started arguing on a regular basis, and that was the beginning of the end for their marriage.

During the week of Runt's 25th birthday, he became a divorcee. Of course, that would put him into serious financial problems. Spiraling debt was overwhelming him, and he started to fall into a deep depression.

On a cold December night a few days before Christmas, he snapped. All his money was spent before he received his paycheck. He had no funds to buy presents for his daughter.

He took out a gun that he had bought for $20 at a pawn shop a couple of years ago. It was an old 22 pistol that hadn't been fired in years. Runt didn't even know how to load it.

The gun fit comfortably inside his right boot. If there was any trouble, he would get it out only for a show of force.

There were no bullets in the chamber.

He asked in a prayer that he would not have to use it.

Suddenly, a thought hit him. "Was it smart to ask for help on a sin that he was about to commit?"

Runt drove the thirty-five miles from the rundown apartment where he lived to the nicest hotel in Kansas City, The Franklin. He hid in the back of the parking lot behind some trees.

Soon, he spotted his mark. Two old ladies stepped out of a brand-new Cadillac. They had parked in the back. It never occurred to them that it might be dangerous there.

Runt took out his teeth and moved his left eye a little in the socket. Those small adjustments made a huge difference in his appearance. He pulled his baseball cap down tight and moved his coat up on his neck. As he made his approach, he put on a pair of old glasses.

"Hello ladies," he said as he walked up to the Cadillac. "How are you doing today?"

Both of the old ladies seemed a little startled, but Runt put them at ease quickly.

"Don't worry, don't worry," he said softly. "I promise I mean no harm. I promise."

The old ladies seemed to sense that he meant it, which he did.

"I would never hurt either one of you," he continued. "I will only trouble you for a minute."

The two women looked at each other, and Runt kept talking.

"I love your coat, ma'am," he said to the lady on his left. "It's beautiful, and it looks great on you."

He turned to the lady on his right.

"And ma'am," he said. "You look really pretty tonight, too."

It was obvious to Runt that the two old ladies could not take their focus off his awkward looking eyeball. Runt kept both hands in his coat pockets.

"I hate to ask you this, but I need your wallets and your jewelry," he said. "Let's make this fast, so you can go on inside. It's cold out here, and I don't want you to get sick."

The two old ladies stared at Runt for about ten seconds.

"It's okay," he added. "This will all be over before you know it. I hate to ask this of you. I really am sorry. Please hand me your wallets and jewelry." Both the old ladies opened their purses and pulled out their wallets. They handed them to Runt just like he asked.

"Ladies," he continued. "I need your jewelry, too."

He noticed that giving up their jewelry kinda made them mad, so he changed gears.

"I'll tell you what," he said. "Keep the jewelry that means something to you.

Just give me what you can."

Both the old ladies smiled. One of them even spoke.

"That's so nice of you," she said. "I feel a lot better."

Runt put the wallets and jewelry in his coat pocket.

"Thank you so much," he said with a smile. "Maybe we will see each other again."

He tipped his hat before he turned and disappeared into the night. The two old ladies scurried inside. They had to tell their story. Nothing that exciting had happened to them in years!

# CHAPTER TWENTY – THREE

One of the old ladies had almost $200 cash in her purse. The other had $20. Runt also obtained six pieces of jewelry. A couple of days later, he gathered the two old ladies' driver's licenses, credit cards, pictures and other items and boxed them up. He addressed the boxes and dropped them off at the post corner two blocks from the hotel where the crime occurred. It was important to get those items back to whom they belonged. He didn't feel that way about their money and jewelry.

The two old ladies argued about what Runt looked like for weeks. The deception he created in his appearance puzzled them. It didn't really matter that much anyway. All they wanted to talk about was how nice he was to them. It was worth the money for the old lady who lost the $200 to have a story to tell.

Runt quickly bought the nicest tricycle he could find for his daughter, Georgia.

It was pink with white stripes. It only costs $65, so he had money left over to buy her some other presents.

The conflict in his soul about what he had done wasn't nearly as bad as what he had expected, but it was the excitement of the whole event that consumed him. He realized that he had finally found a profession where he could excel.

After tying a bow on the tricycle and wrapping the presents, he made his way over to his former in-law's house.

That was where Macy and Georgia now lived.

Runt lugged the tricycle and the presents up to the porch and knocked on the door. His former father-in-law answered.

"What do you want?" he asked.

Runt was very polite. "I have some Christmas presents for Georgia," he answered. "I won't be long. I just want to give them to her."

His father-in-law relented, and Runt walked into the house. Suddenly, Macy walked around the corner. She smiled at him before she spoke.

"Why are you here?" she asked.

Runt was eager to please. "I have some Christmas presents for our daughter."

Just as he said it, Georgia came running in the back door. "Daddy, Daddy!" she yelled, as she jumped into his arms.

Macy was good about the visit. She let Runt play with Georgia for a good two hours. For a little while, all was well.

But it was only for a little while. Soon, reality took over. Macy re-entered the living room. "Georgia, Honey, we have to get ready. We have to go out to dinner with Grandma and Grandpa in thirty minutes."

She stared at Runt. "You need to leave now."

Runt looked up at her and tried to say something. It was something like an "I'm sorry," but he couldn't spit it out.

Georgia acted like any kid would act when she heard that kind of news from her mother.

"I want Daddy!" she said. "I want him!"

Macy kept her cool. She smiled and looked at Runt.

"I understand, Georgia," she said, "but you live here. Your father doesn't make enough money for you to live with him. You would starve."

Her comments cut to the bone, but Runt knew enough about kids to let it go. He bailed Macy out of the argument.

"Honey," he said to Georgia. "Now you know you can't live with me. That's out of the question right now." He stopped talking for a few seconds. "But maybe someday!" He said it under his breath.

Macy picked up on it quickly. "What did you say?" she asked. "I missed that last comment." She said it very sarcastically.

"Oh nothing," he answered. "I was just mumbling."

He hugged Georgia and said his goodbyes. Soon, he started making his exit. Macy followed him out the front door.

"Where did you get the money to buy that tricycle and the presents," she asked. "If you are making more money, you had better be reporting it to my lawyer!"

Runt kept walking over to his truck.

When he got there, he turned around.

Macy was right behind him. She wanted an answer.

"I know people," he answered. "I know people who have old money."

She knew she had no rights to any gifts that were given to Runt. They had gone over all that sort of thing in meetings about the divorce.

Runt got in the truck and drove away.

A tear ran down his cheek. All kinds of thoughts ran through his head, but he couldn't get one thing out of his mind.

"When and where am I going to rob somebody again?"

# CHAPTER TWENTY - FOUR

There was really only one thing that haunted Runt about robbing people. He did not like carrying any kind of a weapon, much less a gun. However, getting caught in a situation where he could not get away was not an option. He knew, somewhere down the line, that he would need it.

He was very careful to never tell anyone about what he was doing as he gathered intelligence on his new vocation. It was obvious what bringing a gun into the equation would mean if he ever ran into the law.

Mr. Derryberry had an old welding shop in his barn. Runt made his way out to the farm early on a Sunday morning.

Quickly, he fired up the machine and welded the trigger of the gun to the frame. Now, there was no way it could ever be fired. The agent of terror that he would use would only be a prop.

Hopefully, if the time ever came, it would matter in court.

On the way back to his apartment, Runt felt a sense of relief. In his mind, he had made progress in his new business. He tried not to think much about what some judge might say about it.

An idea had already occurred to him about his next move. It was a short drive to Kansas City from Olathe. Of course, there were several hotels there.

He would drive his truck to the city and park it in a random lot. Then he would walk. Runt didn't like to run, but he loved to walk. He could walk faster than most people could run. That was the plan for his next job.

He had already learned many things about this new endeavor. He was a blue-collar worker, so it was not uncommon for him to grow a beard. The beard could be shaved away quickly after he got home.

It was the same with his hair. His long, curly red locks draped down out of his baseball cap. They would be gone the next day when he got a haircut.

Glasses also helped. It was easy to pick up a cheap pair almost anywhere. They could be discarded easily.

However, Runt knew what was really advantageous for him. That was adjusting his false teeth and his glass eye.

Friday night rolled around. After he got off work, Runt grabbed a hamburger and took off to Kansas City. Arriving at dusk, he parked his truck about three miles from a row of hotels off the highway.

He waited until after nine o'clock p.m.

It was important, he thought, to make his move as people came back to the hotel for the evening.

As he did on his last robbery, Runt hid behind a tree line and waited for his mark. Soon, the perfect victims drove into the parking lot. It was dark, and the lighting was poor. Mr. and Mrs. Carl Ector were returning from dinner.
The couple drove up in a brand-new Mercedes.

Runt made his approach as the couple climbed out of their car. As he got closer, he could tell they were in their late 60's or early 70's.

As soon as they were both out of the car and the doors were closed, Runt started talking.

"Ma'am, let me help you with your bags," he said. "It's cold out here." Obviously, Mr. and Mrs. Ector were stunned, but Runt quickly eased their minds.

"Don't worry about a thing. I would never hurt you," he said. "Trust need your purse and jewelry ma'am. I also need your wallet, Sir. This is a robbery." Immediately, Mrs. Ector handed him her purse, but Mr. Ector was quick with a response.

"This is ridiculous," he said. "I have never been robbed in my life."

Runt operated like a pro. "I know, Sir," he answered. "I hate to do this to your nice people, but it's my job. Please hand me your wallet."

He already had Mrs. Ector's purse.

"You can't rob me. I'm Carl Ector," he said. "This is an outrage."

Runt was quick with an answer. "I'm sorry Mr. Ector," he answered. "I have to get moving now, please hand me your wallet."

Mr. Ector stood there in defiance, so Runt reached down and pulled the gun half way out of his boot.

"Please Mr. Ector," he said. "Just give me your wallet.

Quickly, Carl Ector handed Runt his wallet.

"Thank you so much. I am so sorry about this. Have a pleasant evening." Runt turned to leave. He had done it again, and the exhilaration was overwhelming! However, he heard something that sounded odd behind him, so he turned around. Carl Ector was doubled over holding his chest.

Suddenly, Mrs. Ector grabbed hold of him.

"Carl! Carl!" she shouted. "What's wrong?"

Runt knew what was wrong. Carl Ector was having a heart attack. He went back over to the car and stabilized Carl on the ground. Mrs. Ector was in shock.

Runt loosened his tie and made him comfortable.

"Mr. Ector," he said. "Help will be here soon, I promise."

Runt got up and ran away. He knew exactly where a phone booth was down the street. Quickly, he got there and called 911.

"There is a man who is having a heart attack in the parking lot at the hotel at 1700 Lewis Highway!" he said calmly.

"Please come quick!"

The lady on the other end of the line started asking questions. Runt calmly answered every one of them.

"Okay," the lady said. "Help is on the way. Who is this?" she asked.

Runt took the receiver and held it away from his face. He looked at it again.

Finally, he spoke back into the phone.

"This is his son, John Ector! Please get here fast!"

As soon as he said it, a fire truck arrived in the parking lot. Immediately, the paramedics went to work on Carl Ector. Runt watched from a distance.

He knew that he was the reason that Carl Ector had the heart attack. He was just hoping that he would be the reason that Carl Ector would survive.

# CHAPTER TWENTY - FIVE

Mule archer stumbled down the front stairs of his front porch as he fetched his Sunday morning paper. He had worked a total of 72 hours during the past week. The Kansas Highway Patrol demanded a 40-hour work week. However, he had supplemented his income by working off duty at three college basketball games and supervising the security for a huge funeral procession.

As he reached down to pick the paper out of his boxwood shrubs, he spilled coffee all over his house shoes.

"Dammit!" he exclaimed loudly.

When he stood up, he spilled more coffee on the paper. "I'll be a...." he stopped himself when he saw his son, Gary, on the front porch staring at him.

"Don't cuss, Daddy!" Gary said to him.

"You better stop. Mama will be mad!" Mule knew Gary was right. "I'm sorry," he answered. "I'll try to do better."

Mule and Gary went back into the house. As they walked in the door Mule's wife and Gary's mother greeted them with a smile on her face.

"Good morning, gentlemen!" she said.

Gary looked at his daddy and scowled.

Mule returned the look and put his right index finger upright across his lips as if to say, "Don't tell on me."

Laura Archer, Mule's wife, cooked a hearty breakfast, and Gary watched TV.

Mule read the paper and drank coffee.

They only had a couple of hours before they had to head off to church.

"Anything interesting in the paper?" Laura asked.

Mule mumbled a faint "No," as he turned the pages. Suddenly, on the third page, something caught his attention.

Courteous Crook Saves Victim's Life read the headline of the story in the top left corner of page three. The headline itself was captivating. The story was even better. Mule read it quickly.

"Listen to this one, Honey!" Mule said to his wife. "Some low-life robs an old man. The old man has a heart attack, and the low-life calls 911. He stays with him until the last second before the paramedics get there, then he runs away. Wow!"

Laura was busy scrambling eggs, but she paid attention to her husband "Nothing would surprise me anymore," she answered. "Where did that happen?"

"Kansas City," Mule responded. "He robbed them at a hotel."

"Have they caught him yet?" Laura asked.

"No," Mule answered. "They haven't caught him. There is nothing in the article about his description. They just talk about how nice he was. That's crazy, isn't it?"

By now, Mule's wife was setting the breakfast table. "I wouldn't know," she said. "I don't know anything about stealing someone's else's money."

Gary sauntered up to the table as the three of them sat down.

"I can't wait to get to there," he said enthusiastically.

Mule laughed. "Why are you so fired up about going to church?" he asked.

Gary was quick with an answer.

"Because I only get to see Uncle Runt and Uncle Kid on Sunday!"

Mule and his wife looked at each other and smiled.

"Well," Laura said. "They both sure need to go to church." The three of them laughed and laughed.

Sure enough, Runt and I were waiting at the church door. Mr. and Mrs. Derryberry were already seated up in the balcony. Runt grabbed Little Gary first and threw him up in the air. It made for a pretty funny scene.

As soon as he landed, I picked him up and threw him in the air, too. We were all late, and the preacher was getting close to starting his sermon. Up the stairs we went and into the balcony. We sat over in what Runt called left center field, the power alley. The preacher looked up at us. He stalled until we all got seated.

Mr. and Mrs. Derryberry couldn't wait to hug on Little Gary. We sat there like we did every Sunday morning. We had been doing it for years.

I knew everybody was watching us, but Runt couldn't help himself.

He poked Little Gary in the ribs and pestered him for an hour. Little Gary took it well, and he kept his mouth shut. He knew his mama would slap him if he talked out loud in church.

When the offering plate came around, everybody knew what to expect. I sat next to the aisle and tried to pass the plate over Runt to Mule. However, Runt would have none of that. He intercepted it.

When it came time to give the offering plate to Mule, Runt did what he did every Sunday. He acted like he was gonna fumble it. Obviously, it made everybody nervous.

Mule was in a tough spot. If he went for the plate, he risked dropping it to the floor. That would be humiliating.

The best thing to do was just to leave Runt alone and hope he wouldn't embarrass all of us.

Eventually, Runt handed the plate to Mule. We were all sweating by then.

Runt looked over at Mrs. Derryberry and winked. She frowned at him before she winked back.

Next came the invitation. I swear the preacher was looking straight at us when he was asking for somebody to come down to meet him. Little Gary started pushing on Runt to go downstairs and join the others who were accepting the preacher's offer, but Runt refused.

After church, we all went over to The Red Barn Cafe to eat lunch. It was always my favorite time of the week.

Mr. and Mrs. Derryberry had Little Gary with them now. They were in the corner spoiling him rotten.

Mule and his wife were discussing something important. It was easy to see how serious they were.

Runt and I sat together at our end of the table.

"Have you done anything exciting lately?" I asked.

Runt looked at me like I was crazy.

"Oh, you know me, Kid," he answered.

"I've got to be the most boring person in the world."

# CHAPTER TWENTY - SIX

I had no idea that runt was robbing people. Nobody did. He might not have been very good in school, but he was very smart when it came to being a thief.

Living under the radar was easy for him. He lived in a small, modest apartment. He drove an old pickup.

He had worked his way up to being a supervisor in his job at the County. If his ex-wife knew of any extra money he was making, she would have her lawyer on it in a minute.

Neither myself nor Mule paid much attention to him. We were too busy living our own lives. We never realized that he was flirting with being on the most wanted list.

I had my own problems. Derryberry

Oil & Gas was now a partnership between Mr. Derryberry and me. I was doing all the work. He just owned all the equipment and had most of the connections. If Mule or Runt would have wanted, they could have been in business with us. However, neither showed any interest.

Once Mule started working for the Pinkertons, he was all in on law enforcement. Runt was different.

Always the rebel, he wanted to do his own thing.

I was making pretty good money, but I was living a pretty mundane life. Mr. and Mrs. Derryberry were getting on up there in age, and it was pretty much just me in the "family" business.

There was another thing that was bothering me. Runt was divorced, but he did have a daughter. Mule was married and had Little Gary. I was jealous of both of them, because I always wanted a family of my own.

I seemed to strike out with every girl I met. Runt would call me "next year's bridegroom" to get under my skin.

"Don't worry about it, Kid!" He would always say it sarcastically. "It ain't what it's all cracked up to be anyway!" He always laughed when he said it.

Mule, on the other hand, was always concerned about my love life. He and Laura were always trying to fix me up with a nice girl.

One night we went out on the town in Kansas City. It felt odd that a married couple would be with a socially awkward wimp and his blind date.

Things started off okay. My date was very pretty, and she had a nice personality. I thought for a moment that this could be a good thing. Mule and his wife kept the conversation going. Laura told her that I ran my own business. I just smiled and kept my mouth shut.

We went to dinner at a famous barbecue place in town called Luther's.

Mule, Runt and I had been going there for years.

The girls didn't realize it, but Luther's was in a pretty bad part of town. We had planned just to be there for dinner and leave.

"I think it is so cool that you and your brothers are so close," she said several times. "My brothers hate each other."

Mule thought it was important to set the record straight.

"We're not really brothers," he responded. "We just grew up together and are like brothers."

My date frowned when he said it.

"Well," she answered, "it seems like you are brothers to me."

"I'm a lot better looking than Mule," I said.

It sounded pretty funny to me, but nobody laughed. My confidence began to waver, so I decided I better just stop trying to be a comedian.

"I think that Mule and I are even closer than brothers. We've been through a lot together."

My date smiled and took a sip of her iced tea. She started nodding her head.

"I can see that," she responded.

We stayed until they were ready to shut down the place. Finally, we started walking to the car. We were all talking about dinner.

"I like that place," my date said. "That was the best barbeque I have ever eaten."

I agreed and turned to seek Mule's assurance. However, he wasn't behind us. Laura grabbed my arm and started walking fast.

"Come on," she said. "We need to go!" She got between me and my date to escort us to the car.

Quickly, she started the ignition and backed the car out of the parking spot.

Before we knew it, she had the car lights shining on the ATM machine outside of Luther's.

There seemed to be an argument going, and Mule was right in the middle of it. Suddenly, Mule dodged a punch, and that was it.

Right there in front of us, Mule Archer pinned a man down on his stomach. He handcuffed him and was reading him his rights. The guy had broken into the ATM machine.

Mule had sensed something funny, and he walked over to check on it. Sure enough, a robbery was in progress. The Midnight Rider had reacted again.

Suddenly, a patrol car pulled up with the lights flashing and the siren blowing. Two police officers jumped out and took over the scene.

My date was stunned. She had never seen anything like that. We all got out of the car.

"I apologize," Mule said "I hate that you guys had to see that. I have to go down to the station. I'm really sorry." He turned to Laura. "I'll get an officer to bring me home, Honey."

It got quiet for a few seconds. Mule shook my date's hand and wished her well before he turned back to his wife.

He didn't even realize that his nose was bleeding and his eye was swollen almost shut.

"That guy," he said, "dang sure wasn't the Courteous Crook!"

# CHAPTER TWENTY - SEVEN

Tom Wayne Rhyner had moved up in the world. He had inherited the family car dealership. He also had done a good job of following his dad's advice.

Every Saturday morning, he made the rounds in the poor sections of town.

Oftentimes, he handed out food, drinks, and sometimes even money. It was important to secure his reputation for his future political aspirations.

He was also quite the womanizer.

Every weekend, it seemed he had a different date on his arm. One night, he was hanging out with some of his friends in a bar named Rooster's. There was a group of women over against the back wall that were making a bunch of noise. Tom Wayne took it upon himself to approach them.

"Ladies! Ladies!" he said politely.

"You're making so much of a fuss nobody can hear themselves think."

He smiled when he said it. Several of the women were very attractive.

One of them spoke up. "Well," she said, "why don't you get some earplugs?

Then, you can think more clearly." Tom Wayne knew how to play the game. "Well, Darlin'," he answered. "I don't have any earplugs on me right now."

The woman smiled. "Well," she said,

"You could buy me a drink. That might quiet us down a little."

Tom Wayne held out his arm in a way that asked her to take him as an escort.

As they walked to the bar the other women heckled them. Neither Tom Wayne nor his new friend seemed to care.

When they sat down, Tom Wayne started the conversation. "What is a beautiful lady like you doing in a place like this?"

The beautiful woman was smitten.

"Well," she said, "maybe I am looking for a friend like you."

The conversation continued. Tom Wayne was the first to introduce himself formally.

"My name's Tom Wayne Rhyner," he said. "Maybe you have heard of Rhyner Auto Mart?"

The woman didn't flinch. "No," she answered. "Never heard of it."

Tom Wayne pressed on. "Well," he said. "what's your name?"

"My name is Macy Suggs."

Immediately, she realized her mistake and corrected it. "Well," she said, "my last name isn't Suggs, any more. I'm divorced."

Tom Wayne scrunched his eyebrows down. His eyes darted to the left, then to the right.

"I know a guy with the last name of Suggs," he said. "Do you know Runt Suggs?"

Macy seemed embarrassed. "How do you know Runt?" she asked.

Tom Wayne couldn't contain himself.

"Well," he said, "first of all, I had to whoop him a couple of times. He's the biggest punk I know!"

Macy seemed to come alive. "What do you mean?" she asked. "What do you have against Runt?"

"His mouth is what I have against him," Tom Wayne answered. "He thinks that he's all that. I had to take him down a couple of notches. He couldn't fight his way out of a paper bag, though. He takes off running when things get a little tough."

Macy was unamused. She was down on Runt more than anyone, but he was still her daughter's father.

"He's my ex-husband," she said.

She turned away. She thought Tom Wayne Rhyner would have nothing else to do with her, but she was wrong.

"T imagine that was pretty insulting on my part, wasn't it?" Tom Wayne responded. "I don't like him, though.

You figured that out, huh?"

Macy composed herself before she looked at Tom Wayne. Finally, she turned to him and spoke. "He is very good to our daughter. He loves her very much. I should have never married him.

He never fit into my social class, but I was young and foolish."

Tom Wayne was smart enough to shut his mouth and listen for a while. Macy continued talking. "It's not that I hate him or anything. I just have no more romantic interest in him. It's all in the past. We have a child together. I have to work with him."

Tom Wayne smiled. He was very attracted to Macy. A few seconds crept by as the two of them looked at each other.

"Would you like to dance?" Tom Wayne asked.

Without saying a word, Macy stretched out her left hand. Tom Wayne escorted her to the small dance floor.

They danced the rest of the night away.

Runt's name never came up again that evening.

# CHAPTER TWENTY - EIGHT

The telephone rang at my house early Saturday morning. "Kid," the voice on the other end said. "It's time to get up!"

After rubbing my eyes and clearing the cobwebs out of my head, I realized who was trying to aggravate me.

"Runt," I responded. "What time is it?

He didn't hesitate. "Get up Kid!" he answered. "It's six a.m."

Mule and I were always astounded at how it seemed that Runt never slept. He was always up at an unimaginable hour.

He also stayed up late at night. A lot of the times he would be out carousing.

Sure enough, the clock said 6:05.

"What are you doing tonight?" Runt asked.

"No big plans," I answered. "What's up?"

"Well Kid," Runt said. "I'm loaning my pickup out to a guy I work with at the county. He has a big date. I'm going to meet him up on North Crider Road in Kansas City at the Tastee Freeze. Can you come get me at 7:30? We can go drink some beer!"

He seemed so excited.

"Sure," I responded. "I'll see you at then."
I spent the rest of the day working on a deal with Mr. Derryberry. Runt spent the rest of the day studying.

He knew exactly where to go and what to do that night. He had used his downtime in a local bar asking where the biggest poker game in Kansas City would be held. It was to be downtown at the Sandstone Hotel on 6th Street.

Word was that it was in room 602.

Runt was nervous all day, but he was also excited. He had prepared for three clothing changes. Everything he needed was in his backpack. He knew his exact route.

At 5:00, he took off. First, it was a four-mile hike to the bus station. He got off the bus a couple of blocks away from the Sandstone. Soon, he was standing in the shadows of the building watching the people come and go.

Dusk fell right at 6:30 p.m. Runt slowly made his way inside. He waited until he saw a mark that might fit his agenda.

He kept his distance as he watched a man in a camel hair jacket get on the elevator.

Soon, Runt was positioned just inside the staircase. Right at 7:00, the first person walked out of room 602. Runt waited patiently. Sure enough, it was the man in the camel hair jacket.

Runt followed him out to his car. It just happened to be parked in the back of the parking lot. "Sir," he said. "I'm sorry to bother you."

The man in the camel hair jacket seemed a little stunned. He had a defeated look on his face.

"This is a stickup," Runt said with no emotion. "I need your wallet."

The man in the camel hair jacket laughed. "What?" he asked. "You're kidding, right?"

"I'm not kidding, Sir," Runt responded.

"I need all your valuables."

Runt reached down and grabbed the .22 pistol. He did not point it at the man in the camel hair jacket. He just held it down at his side.

Soon Runt had all the man's valuables.

"I apologize for vandalizing you, Sir,"

Runt said. "I wish I didn't need to do this. I wish you the best."

Suddenly, Runt was gone. On the way down the dark sidewalk, he was taking off his jacket and hat. Into the trash they went. His cheezy, fake mustache was gone, too. He just threw it on the ground. Along the way, he put his teeth back into his mouth.

As he made it downtown, he felt the momentum. An elderly couple were trying to get inside their car.

"How are you guys doing today?" he asked them. "Can I help you?"

The old man was pretty angry. "Darn it," he said. "I can't get this door open!" Runt walked over beside him. "Let me help you," he said calmly.

Soon the door was open, so Runt moved in for the close. He needed to move quickly and get on his way.

"Sir," he said. "I need your wallet. This is a robbery."

The old man was stunned. His wife didn't even know what was happening.

Before you knew it, Runt had the old man's wallet and his watch.

"I need her purse, too, Sir," Runt added.

"Well, you're sure a greedy son-of-a-gun, aren't you?" the old man asked.

"Mama," he said, "let him have your purse," She did exactly as he said.

"I will try to make this up to you someday, Sir," Runt said. "I apologize for doing this to you."

He actually tipped his hat as he scampered away. Again, he stripped off his jacket and baseball cap and deposited them into a dumpster.

Runt galloped over three miles to his next stop. Tom's Quick Serve was positioned perfectly. Before you knew it, Runt walked right up on an old farmer filling up his black, Chevrolet two-ton truck.

This time, Runt pulled his gun quickly.

Artfully, he hid it from anyone to see but the farmer. He was in no mood for small talk.

"Sir" he said. "This is a hold up. I'm sorry, but I need all your money and valuables."

The old farmer was in a good mood. He rolled his eyes. "Son," he said. "I'll give you anything you want. Just don't hurt me, Okay?"

"I don't want to hurt anyone, Sir," Runt answered.

The old man handed over his wallet and emptied his pockets before looking down at his watch. "My wife gave me this watch before she died," he said. "Do you really have to have it, too?"

Runt thought about things quickly.

He already had his biggest haul to date.

There was no reason to be greedy. He needed to make an exit.

"Keep your watch, Sir," he said. "I'm sorry to rob you."

Runt turned to leave. Suddenly, the old man lunged at Runt and grabbed his arm. Runt swung back quickly and shook him off. There was no way the old man could catch Runt as he ran away.

However, someone actually fighting back stunned him.

Again, Runt ditched the black windbreaker into a trash can. After a four-mile walk, he stepped into the Tastee Freeze bathroom. The poker player in the camel hair jacket had almost four hundred dollars on him.

The old couple in the parking lot had a hundred and twenty. The farmer who talked Runt into allowing him to keep the watch had five twenty-dollar bills.

The cash haul alone was a total of $620.

That didn't include the jewelry.

I pulled up right on time at 7:30. Runt opened the door and jumped into my new pickup.

"Where we going?" he asked. "I'm ready to roll tonight."

We drove along and talked and talked and talked. Neither of us could say as much as we wanted to say before the other interrupted. After three beers, there was finally a lull in the conversation.

"Hey Kid," Runt said, "this is like old times, isn't it?" I nodded my head.

"You know," he added. "I'm a little short on cash tonight. I hope you understand."

I nodded my head again. I had heard him say that a million times.

# CHAPTER TWENTY - NINE

Mule archer got out of bed at 5:45 a.m. It was Saturday morning. He was such a creature of habit that he couldn't sleep in like a normal person. That would throw a kink into his psyche.

He threw on his house shoes and grabbed a cup of coffee. Next, he would walk out in the front yard to pick up his paper. He did the same thing every day he wasn't on active duty.

Keeping a low profile was important today. Laura, his wife, was on the warpath. As usual, they were having a financial crisis. Mule got an earful about how he didn't make enough money during every conversation with her.

This short period of time that she was asleep gave him some peace.

It was windy and cold. Mule looked down both ends of the street before he went back into the house. As he opened the paper, Laura walked into the living room. That was odd. She never got up that early.

The picture of Mule holding the paper set her off again.

"That newspaper cost $10 per month.

We could use that money a better way."

She said it with venom in her voice.

Mule didn't respond. He went through the paper looking for anything to do with crime. He found it on the fourth page. Police Concerned About Series of Robberies, one headline read. Mule dug into the story.

"I have to buy groceries today," Laura said. "I need a haircut, and I think I have a nail in one of my tires."

She bent over and put her hands on her knees. Soon, she was crying. When she stood up again, the rant continued.

"And we have to go out to my mother's birthday party tonight downtown. How are we gonna pay for it, Mule?" It took Mule five minutes to read the article. "Can't anybody get a decent description?" he asked.

"Description of what?" Laura asked.

"Whoever is robbing these people,"

Mule answered. "This is ridiculous.

Nobody can get any kind of an ID on this guy. One day he is tall. The next day he is short. One time he has a beard. The next time he is clean shaven."

Laura didn't care about the Courteous Crook. "I'm ready to go home to my mom and dad's house," she said frantically. *I can't live like this, Mule.

We're just above vagrants. I'm telling you; you need to make more money." Laura started drinking her coffee.

"And," she continued, "I can't take all this violence. Every time I turn around, you're wrestling with some criminal.

It's insane!"

Mule folded the paper and set it on the table. He had already decided not to get into an argument with her. He had complained about her spending habits many times before. It did no good.

"It wouldn't matter if she was married to the richest man in the world," he thought to himself. "She would spend it all. He would be broken, too."

"Daddy said Little Gary and I could come home," Laura continued. "I'm serious, Mule. I can't take it anymore. I want a divorce."

As bad as it had been in the past, Mule had never heard that before. It hurt for a minute, but he did entertain the thought that it could be a positive. He never thought his life could be in such a mess.

The day passed and the family met Laura's parents and sisters at a restaurant in Kansas City. Not a word was spoken on the way to the party.

There was some laughing and joking at the end of the table, but it was very somber on the Archer's end. Mule started fighting with his chicken fried steak. He couldn't figure out how to cut it.

Laura's dad was a good 'ole boy who was always kind. "Mule," he hollered across the table, "have you been putting any of those bad guys away?" he asked.

Mule just laughed. "We're trying," he answered. "We're trying our best."

Laura's dad was observing the tension between his daughter and her husband.

Suddenly, the oddest thing happened.

A couple was seated only a few tables away from the birthday party. As he always did, Mule paid attention. The man that was seated at the table looked familiar. Mule selectively peeked at him when he got a chance.

"I have to go to the bathroom," Mule said.

Nobody seemed to care. He went straight to the house phone and called his office.

"Grab every picture you can of him," he said. "I'm pretty sure he was the armed guy in the Learman Bank robbery. Get over here now in an unmarked car. I'll meet you out front." Mule calmly went back to the table.

The party was about to break up, but Mule needed to stall for time.

"Let's get some dessert," he said. "It's not right to have a birthday party without a birthday cake."

He looked over at Laura. She was staring off into space.

The cake arrived just about the same time as the sheriff in the unmarked car.

Mule saw the officer as he walked in the door. He was in plain clothes.

"Man, I drank too much coffee tonight," Mule said. "I'll be right back." He made his way to the bathroom.

The other officer followed. They filed through the photos in the stall.

One picture jumped out of the file.

"That's him," Mule said. "He's sitting right out there in the restaurant.

The other officer spoke up. "We have a positive ID on him," he said. "We can pick him up right now."

The look on Mule's face told the whole story. He knew how the next step would go over with Laura, but he also knew what he had to do.

Quickly, the two peace officers made their plan. Mule walked back to the table. He knew he needed to hurry.

Mule asked for the check, and he put it on his credit card. The family got up to leave. Mule stayed behind. He waited until everyone had walked out the front door.

The other officer walked towards the couple's table. Mule was standing five feet away-

Suddenly, the man identified in the picture figured it out. He broke for the door, but he had no chance.

Mule tackled him. The bad guy was handcuffed in less than a minute.

Instinctively, Mule looked for his wife.

She was standing outside the door watching through the front window.

Their eyes met. Suddenly, she turned and walked away.

The panic in the restaurant didn't faze the two lawmen. They had him in the unmarked car in no time.

"I'll be at the office in thirty minutes,"

Mule said. "I have to take care of my family."

Mule Archer turned back to the parking lot. He looked for Laura and Little Gary, but he couldn't find them.

He walked out to where he had parked the car, but he couldn't find them. Laura and Little Gary were gone.

# CHAPTER THIRTY

The relationship between Macy Suggs and Tom Wayne Rhyner was making things very complicated. It wasn't that Runt cared that much about Macy being romantically involved with another man. He had pretty much accepted that the relationship with his ex-wife was over for good. It would also probably be a good thing for him financially.

The problem was that he just hated Tom Wayne Rhyner with a passion. Of course, Tom Wayne hated him right back.

There was also the issue of their daughter, Georgia. Like any divorced dad, Runt was as jealous as a mother pig guarding her piglets. Every time their paths crossed; the tension was off the charts.

Runt would show up at Macy's parents' house with presents for Georgia.

The gifts weren't elaborate. Mainly, he bought her clothes, shoes, school supplies and the like. It made him feel fulfilled. At least, it helped make him feel a little more fulfilled. The truth was that he was dying inside.

Every time he would show up with something for Georgia, Macy would ask him how he got the money to buy it. She knew it got under his skin, but she always persisted. She was a good person, but divorce can bring out the worst in people. It certainly did to both Macy and Runt.

Runt always gave the same answer.

"It's a gift from someone who cares about her." Runt would always say.

"A gift from whom?" Macy would always ask.

"It's a gift from somebody who has a lot of old money," Runt would respond.

"It's none of your business."

"It is my business," Macy would say.

"I deserve to know. I'm her mother." Of course, Runt would never give up the source.

One Sunday afternoon, Macy went to the store to buy groceries. She was minding her own business and was enjoying a pretty good day. Tom Wayne had taken her and Georgia to church that morning. She was impressed that he paid as much attention to her daughter as he did to her. He knew she liked that.

As she smelled a tomato in the produce section, a thought hit her.

"Tom Wayne is pretty sweet on me. We might just have a future."

It was funny. She hadn't really given their relationship that much thought.

She enjoyed his company a little, but she enjoyed his money a lot. Tom Wayne Rhyner came from a wealthy family. If she stayed with him, she and Georgia would always be financially secure.

However, she wasn't sure she could ever really love him. She didn't show it, but she still loved Runt. It was just impossible for her to co-exist with him.

"How you doing, Macy?" a low, rough voice asked.

Macy dropped the tomato and came back to consciousness. She had slipped away for a moment.

After gathering her composure, she answered. "I'm good. How are you, Mule?"

Mule Archer was grocery shopping, too. By coincidence, their paths had crossed. They had never been close friends. She was friendly with Mule's wife, Laura. However, after her divorce from Runt, they hadn't been in contact.

After a few awkward seconds, Mule spoke. "How is Georgia?" he asked.

"She's fine," Macy answered. "She's fine."

"I miss Laura," Macy said. "How is she doing?" She was very aware that she didn't say she missed Mule.

"Laura's fine," he answered. "She went back to work. Did you know that?" Macy was taken aback. "No," she said.

"I didn't know that."

It got quiet again and very awkward.

Mule decided it was time for him to move on.

"I have to go," he said. "It was good to see you."

However, Macy Suggs wasn't ready to let him leave yet. She had some questions.

"Mule," she started, "how often do you see Runt?"

"Not very often," Mule answered.

"He's busy. I'm busy. We're not kids anymore."

Macy couldn't contain herself. "He brings Georgia a lot of stuff that I know he can't afford. Does he have a job that I don't know about? If he does and my lawyer finds out, he's in big trouble." Mule stepped back into the conversation. "What kind of stuff?" he asked.

"Dresses, books, girl things," Macy answered. "He always says it's a gift from someone with old money. That's old man Derryberry, isn't it Mule?"

Mule was confused. "Well, I don't know," he answered. "I just don't know." By now, Macy was ready to go on the warpath. "If he has another job, I am entitled to my part of his earnings. That was the agreement."

"But if it's a gift, he doesn't have to give it to you, right?" Mule asked.

Macy nodded her head. Mule was just learning about this divorce business.

"I'm no fool!" Macy all but screamed.

"I'm telling you, Mule, if he is holding out on me, I will make sure he goes to jail." It was obvious that she was as mad as a hornet.

Suddenly, the chance meeting went from friendly to defensive. Mule leaned back from Macy. He looked away.

Finally, he looked her straight in the eye.

"I heard you are dating Tom Wayne Rhyner," he said.

"I am," Macy answered. "And it's none of your business."

That rudeness was unbecoming of Macy.

"I'm sorry," she said quickly. "That was terrible of me. I'm sorry." She started crying.

Mule took a deep breath. "It's okay, Macy," he said. "I understand." Mule started to walk away, but he stopped and turned around.

"I'll try to get to the bottom of this question for you," he said. Macy nodded in return.

Mule Archer made his way out of the grocery store and to his car. He would find somewhere else today to buy what he needed.

On the way home he could not get the conversation out of his mind. He went into analytical mode. He squinted his eyes tightly together. He rubbed his head. A thought ran through his mind.

"About six foot tall," he thought to himself. "He had a charming personality, very friendly and courteous."

Mule kept driving. "Could it be?" he asked himself.

"No, it couldn't be."

# CHAPTER THIRTY - ONE

Mule and I laughed all the way down to the water. We watched Runt jump in the river and take a bath. I didn't think he would ever get the puke out of his red hair. Pretty soon though, he was swimming around like Mark Spitz.

"Come on in!" he yelled. "This feels great."

It was about 95 degrees that day.

Before I knew it, Mule jumped in with him. I stayed up on the bank.

"That was sure a heck of a plan, Kid!" Runt cried. "You knew that was gonna happen, didn't you? You're sorry!"

Mule was trying to float like a log, but he wasn't having much success. "Those cows just knew it was you, Runt," he said. "I guess they thought you were a portable outhouse or something." Runt sent a wave of water over at him after he said it.

I watched the two of them lounge in the water. Sure enough, Runt started in on me.

"Come on, Kid," he said. "Jump in!

What are you waiting for?"

I didn't know what to say, but I knew I had to answer. I just blurted out the first thing I thought. "I don't want to get my clothes wet!" I yelled.

"Shooot!" Runt answered. "I ain't got no clothes on. Come on, jump in!" I started to get up and walk back uphill to the truck.

"Let's get back to work!" I yelled down at the two swimmers.

"You're scared, aren't you?" Runt asked loudly. "Are you worried that a water moccasin is gonna bite you on the butt?" I couldn't help but notice that Mule was laughing.

"I ain't scared," I answered. "I just don't want to get into that dirty old river."

"Well," Runt screamed, "all you gotta do is relax your body and wave your arms. See how I'm doing it." I stopped and turned around. Runt decided to add to his lecture. "If you can tread water, you can swim. Watch me!" I have to admit that I was paying close attention. Runt swirled around in the water. Then, all of a sudden, he went under.

At first, Mule and I didn't think anything of it. A minute or so went by.

There was no sign of Runt. Another minute went by. Again, there was no sign of Runt.

"Where is he?" Mule asked. You could tell he was a little panicky.

Another minute or so went by. Mule went under water to look for him. It didn't take ten seconds before his head was back up out of the water.

I stripped down to my underwear. I was scared to death, but I knew I had to help. Mule went under again. Ten seconds later, his head popped out of the water again.

I jumped into the river. When I went under, my eyeballs popped out of socket and I lost my underwear. My nose and ears flooded. The next thing I knew, my head was out of the river. I started circling my arms like Runt told me to do. Soon, I relaxed and calmed down.

I decided to go under again to try to find Runt, but it was useless. The river was so dark I couldn't see anything. My head popped out of the water.

"Where is he?" I asked Mule. We both thought the worst possible thing. We thought Runt was a goner.

Suddenly, a dirt clod hit the water right by my head. Another one hit a foot away from Mule. Then, a slow barrage of ammo started coming our way. It was Runt. He was throwing mud balls at us from across the river.

"Come on, Kid!" Mule hollered. "Let's go over there and whoop him!"

Off we went to the other side. Neither of us would admit to the relief we felt.

Mule made it over to the other side first. I lagged behind, but I moved pretty good. It was one of the proudest moments in my life. I had finally learned how to swim!

# CHAPTER THIRTY - TWO

Macy Suggs was very unhappy. She and Georgia still lived with her parents.

Financially, she was fine. Her parents provided great care. It was just that she felt like she was wasting her life away.

She always blamed her troubles on Runt. He swept her off her feet when they were young and married her. Then, he turned out to be a big disappointment.

`Bitterness had overcome her, and she couldn't get past it. Even though she really didn't need it, she tried to get every penny out of him. She would never even consider to ratchet down the pressure. It really bothered her that Runt always seemed to have extra cash, and it made her intensely jealous and bitter. Nobody understood it. She was dating the richest guy in town, Tom Wayne Rhyner, but that didn't matter to Macy. She wanted to see Runt suffer.

Of course, Tom Wayne played right into the drama.

There was no question that Macy was one of the most beautiful women in town. Her long hair and voluptuous figure caught almost everyone's attention. That just made her feel more like an underachiever. Now she had a chance to turn it completely around if her new boyfriend was interested in taking things into the long term.

Don't think for a minute that Tom Wayne wasn't aware of how these events were upsetting Runt. It was obviously another way for Tom Wayne to get a leg up on the rivalry.

One night during dinner, Macy couldn't help herself. She had thought of a way to find out the truth about Runt and his extra money.

"Don't you have some contacts that can find out things?" she asked Tom Wayne.

Tom Wayne was a little confused.

"What do you mean?" he asked.

"You know," Macy responded. "Can't you hire somebody to follow Runt around and see what he is doing to get that extra money?"

Tom Wayne wanted to make sure he impressed Macy. "Sure," he said. "I can probably do that for you."

He carved the steak he was eating and took a big bite. "It'll cost you though."

He winked at her as he said it. Macy shrugged it off as if he didn't say it.

The thought hit her that she might be getting in a little over her head.

Tom Wayne thought about her request for a week. "How can I use this to my advantage?" he wondered.

The same idea kept coming back to him. "What about Mule?" he thought.

"He's in law enforcement, and I know he needs the money. This could be really good!"

The following Saturday morning at ten o'clock, Tom Wayne started to work on his plan. He called Mule on the phone. When Mule answered, the awkwardness of the situation was obvious.

"Mule," Tom Wayne said. "I'm looking for a man like you to do a job for me." Mule was skeptical, but he listened.

"If you're interested, it pays very well.

It won't take too much work. I just need some basic information. Do you think you are interested?"

Immediately, Mule started having reservations. How in the world could he go to work for Tom Wayne Rhyner?"

"I don't know," he answered. "I'm pretty busy. I'm not sure I have the time."

Tom Wayne was quick with an answer.

"Oh, you have the time," he said. "You won't make this kind of money doing law enforcement work. But if you're not interested, I can get someone else."

"What's the job?" Mule asked.

Tom Wayne had prepared for that question. "I have to have a commitment first," he answered. "If you go to work for me there will be some ground rules."

Mule had heard enough. "I'm not interested," he said. "I have to get going."

He hung up the phone without thanking Tom Wayne for the offer. As soon as he was finished, his wife, Laura, was standing next to him. She wanted to know what the phone call was about.

"Was that a job offer?' she asked. "It sure sounded like it was."

Mule got up and tried to walk away.

"No," he answered. "It was just some guy wanting information."

That didn't stop her from nagging.

"That was a job offer, wasn't it?" she asked. "Why didn't you take it? You know how much we need the money." She lectured Mule all the way to the door. He got in his car and drove away.

Things were really getting tense in their marriage. Mule was beginning to think she was really going to leave him.

On the way to his moonlighting job as a security officer, he worried. Going to work for Tom Wayne Rhyner violated everything he believed. It made him sick to his stomach.

However, he knew he needed the money. His instincts told him that Tom Wayne would pay well, very well. It was just that he knew the truth. If he went to work for the enemy, it would be like selling his soul.

# CHAPTER THIRTY -THREE

The next morning, Mule got up and made his way down to the Highway Patrol headquarters.

He couldn't get his mind off the phone call from Tom Wayne Rhyner. It was hard to figure out what to do about the situation.

"Should I tell Runt and Kid?" he thought. "Should I take the job?" He struggled to come up with an answer. Slowly, he made his way to the front door. Retrieving the mail every day was always a labor of love for him.

He turned the key and opened the box.

What he saw startled him. His mailbox was packed.

Mule couldn't help but to look around to see if anybody was watching. There was no way he could carry all the letters in two hands. He would have to use a box. Slowly, he pulled one envelope out of the mailbox and opened it. It was addressed only to "Mule."

The only thing the letter contained was one message. In big black letters it read Mule, your days are numbered!

If it was meant to scare Mule, it worked. Quickly, he put the letter back into the envelope and stuffed it into the mailbox.

"Fame," he thought to himself. "I hate it."

He knew many of the other letters in the box had the same kind of message. As the years had passed, Mr. Derryberry's prediction had proven to be accurate.

Mule turned left and bumped into his supervisor, Captain Jesse Polland. Mule apologized for the awkwardness of Two grown men making physical contact.

"I'm sorry, Sir," he said. "I didn't see you."

Captain Polland wasn't fazed. "No problem," he answered. "I need to talk to you. Can you follow me down to my office?"

The captain didn't wait for a response.

He simply turned around and headed down the hallway. Mule followed him.

The captain opened the door and allowed Mule to walk into the office.

After that, he closed the door. As he sat down behind his desk, he adjusted the toothpick in his mouth. He took a long look at Mule who was standing on the other side of the desk.

"Sit down, Lieutenant Archer," the captain told Mule. "Relax, you're not in trouble."

Mule sighed as he obeyed the order. It had already been a long day, and he was just getting started.

"Mule," the captain started, "we have a tough situation down in Franklin County. There's an old farmer down there named Johnny Radford. They're foreclosing on his home place. It's been in his family for over a hundred years.

He's not taking it well, and the locals think he is dangerous."

Captain Polland stared at Mule. Mule stared back.

"My secretary has all the details. Go down there and settle this."

Mule stood up. "Yes Sir," he answered.

He turned and walked away. On the way out the door, he smiled. It was an honor to go on a mission like this one.

It took an hour to drive down to Johnny Radford's farm. Mule drove into the gravel entryway from the road. It was 2:00 in the afternoon. The unmarked Ford Crown Victoria car was creeping along as Mule approached the barn. There was an old abandoned house about fifty yards away.

Mule got out of the car. He saw no one.

"Mr. Radford," he yelled. "This is Mule Archer. I'm from the Sheriff's Department."

A couple of minutes went by. Finally, Johnny Radford walked out of the barn. He was carrying a rifle. He was also wearing a gun belt that housed a revolver.

"Mule Archer," he yelled. "I read about you in the papers."

Mule and Johnny Radford stared at each other. Mule broke the ice.

"Mr. Radford, you know I have no beef with you, but you have to leave the farm. It's over."

The two men continued to stare at each other. Again, Mule initiated the conversation.

"Mr. Radford, you need to put that rifle down. You don't want that kind of trouble and neither do I."

Johnny Radford adjusted his feet and raised the rifle into firing position.

"Don't do that Mr. Radford!" Mule yelled.

"Put the rifle down!"

All the way until that very second, Mule never took Johnny Radford seriously. He just thought the whole thing was a bluff. However, the sense of urgency suddenly engulfed him.

Johnny Radford pointed the rifle straight at Mule.

"Don't do it!" Mule yelled.

Mule zeroed in on Johnny Radford's trigger finger. His vision was as sharp as an eagle. It looked like Johnny was actually going to shoot the rifle.

Mule pulled his gun and fired. It only took one shot, and Johnny Radford went down. Mule ran over to him and started applying first aid. It didn't matter, though. The bullet went right through Johnny Radford's chest.

# CHAPTER THIRTY - FOUR

"Dang it mule, why didn't you just shoot him in the leg? Why did you have to kill him?" Runt Suggs didn't care much about being sympathetic.

Oddly enough, that was the first time that thought had even entered Mule's mind. "I just reacted," he answered. "I tried to get him to drop the rifle, but he wouldn't do it. I really thought he was gonna shoot me."

I have to admit that I was doing all I could to stay out of the conversation. I felt it was just my job to sit in the corner of Runt's little apartment and observe.

Runt got up and walked to his fridge.

He had plenty of beer. That was why we decided to meet there. He brought everyone a brew, but Mule refused.

He was very upset about what had happened at Johnny Radford's farm, and he wasn't interested in alcohol.

Mule put his head into his hands. "This will be the final straw for Laura and me," he said. "She's had enough of all this." Runt put all the beer away. He realized there should be no drinking. He went back over to his best friend who was sitting in a chair.

"I'm sorry, Mule," he said. "I shouldn't have said that."

Runt walked around the room a couple of times. "You know Mule, there are other things you can do for a living.

Have you ever thought about that?" Of course, Mule never had thought about that. Ever since he started working for the Pinkertons, law enforcement had been his passion.

"I'm not gonna do anything else," answered. "You know that, Runt." It got quiet in the room. A feeling of despair overwhelmed all three of us. A thunderclap went off outside that made us jump a little. It broke the tension, and we all smiled at the same time.

I decided that it might be time for me to add to the conversation. "Have you guys heard the latest about Tom Wayne Rhyner?" I asked.

Immediately, Mule's head snapped to attention. Runt, on the other hand, just sat there. He said nothing. I'm sure that he thought I was gonna tell him that Tom Wayne and Macy were now engaged.

"He's opening a bank," I said. "It's going to be over on 43rd Street. He's already bought the land and the building." It was obvious that Mule was stunned.

Runt had already heard about it.

"Turns out that he's been going to banking school," I added. "Nobody knew it."

"He's gonna save the town from all its financial troubles," Runt mumbled under his breath.

Mule didn't know what to think.

"When did all this go down?" he asked.

"I never heard anything about it."

"He bought it last week. You gonna put your money in Tom Wayne Rhyner's bank, Mule?" I asked.

I couldn't help but snicker when I said it, but I'll never forget the look on Mule's face. I thought he was gonna get up and whoop me.

All the talk about Tom Wayne took the edge off the real problem of the moment, though. Mule had just shot a man dead. It was self-defense, but he was gonna have to go through the process with the Highway Patrol brass.

For quite a while, he would be bound to a desk. Runt and I knew that was gonna drive him crazy.

There was also the emotional toll it would take. The three of us were so close you would have thought Runt or myself had shot Johnny Radford. We hurt right along with Mule. My stomach was churning.

Runt was really upset. He was fidgeting and walking around the room.

Suddenly, an odd look crossed his face.

He realized something none of us had thought of before.

"The newspapers are gonna be all over this, Mule. You know that, don't you?" Mule hadn't been thinking about the newspapers. He had been thinking about Johnny Radford and his family.

All of a sudden, he realized that what Runt said was true.

"Oh my gosh," he mumbled. "You're right. It's only a matter of time."

Runt was adamant about what to do.

"We better get a plan together on how to deal with this. We probably won't be able to keep your name out of the papers, but we need to try to keep them from publishing another picture of you."

It was then that I asked a stupid question. "Why do we need to keep his picture out of the paper?" I asked.

Mule and Runt both looked at me in disgust. "Come on, Kid," Runt answered.

"He's the Midnight Rider, that's why.

Every wanna-be gunslinger in the country will be out to get him."

# CHAPTER THIRTY - FIVE

All this activity was making Runt very nervous. His best friend, Mule, had just gunned down a man who pointed a rifle right at his head. His arch enemy, Tom Wayne Rhyner, was going into the banking business. Also, he was pretty sure Tom Wayne was getting ready to propose to his ex-wife. That's a lot of turmoil.

However, Runt had a lot of ongoing business of his own. His antics as the Cordial Crook had wielded him a pretty good stash of cash. The money was spread out around his apartment.

He had $500 in a sock in the bottom drawer of his dresser. Another $500 was hidden strategically underneath the sink. In the pull drawers at the bottom of the refrigerator, he had another $500. Finally, underneath his bed frame, still another $2,000 was carefully hidden. He kept all the rest as petty cash.

Runt had made it a point to work Saturdays for Kid and Mr. Derryberry.

It would always be a cush job for him, and he knew it. It also made for a good cover.

There was a problem though. It didn't pay enough. The more his makeshift savings account blossomed, the more he knew he needed to expand it. But there was a deeper reason for him to steal again. He loved the high that it gave him.

Runt knew it was important to plan everything down to the last detail.

There must be protection against failure. However, he had no idea that Tom Wayne Rhyner was going to try to get Mule to follow him.

Two weeks after the shooting in Franklin County, Runt was ready to strike again. It was a quiet Sunday morning. He got up early and drove his pickup to Overland, Kansas. There, he parked at a Walmart and walked to the bus station where he caught a ride to downtown Kansas City. The last bus back to Overland left at 5:45 p.m. Runt Suggs had exactly eight hours to make his sweep of crime across the city.

In his backpack, he had everything he needed. First, he walked six miles north to the wealthiest part of the city. The Catholic Church on Roosevelt Street would start mass at 11:00 a.m. sharp. Runt positioned himself on the outskirts of the parking lot.

Mr. and Mrs. Richard Patterson had just parked in the back of the church. As they got out of their car, Runt made his move.

Strategically, he caught Mr. Patterson before he could close the car door. Mrs. Patterson was still sitting in her seat.

She had not even gotten to a point to exit the car.

"Sir," Runt said, "please cooperate and this will be over quickly."

Mr. Patterson had no idea what he meant. Runt's plan was going well. He had his victim pinned between the car door and the car.

"Don't be alarmed," he said. "You aren't in danger. I just need your cash, that's all."

Mr. Patterson suddenly figured out what was happening, but he couldn't move. By now, Runt had hold of the door, and Mr. Patterson was trapped.

"I really hate to do this to you," Runt continued. "I really mean it, but I need all your cash."

Mr. Patterson locked eyes with Runt. That was exactly what Runt wanted. His left eye was tilted out of socket. There was also a huge black mark underneath the eye. It totally dominated Mr. Patterson's attention. He didn't even notice anything else about Runt's appearance.

Mrs. Patterson started talking on the other side of the car. "Richard," she said.

"What's going on over there?"

"Nothing Honey" he answered. "Just be quiet."

Richard Patterson reached into his pocket and pulled out his wallet. He pulled out all the cash and handed it to Runt.

"Thank you so much, Sir," Runt said.

Then he was gone in an instant. Richard Patterson was going to give all of the $300 in cash to the church.

Runt took off down the sidewalk.

He already knew where the trash cans would be located to dump the cowboy hat and the denim jacket he was wearing. Before he knew it, he was almost two miles away. The next stop was a restaurant called Billie's.

The same strategy was used there.

Runt pinned an old woman between her car door and her car. She was by herself.

People were getting into and out of their cars as close as twenty feet away.

However, it looked like an older lady and her son were simply talking. Runt stole almost $100 cash from her. She put up no defense. All she remembered was that the robber had no teeth.

The Cordial Crook was on a roll.

He hopped on a bus and was back downtown before he knew it. He looked at his watch. He needed to finish his day.

Runt made his way over to a movie theatre. He waited until the perfect mark and his wife made it to their car at the back of the parking lot. Suddenly, Runt skipped to the car. When the man tried to back up, Runt slipped behind the car and made contact. The thud startled the young couple.

Jimmy Rosenberg slammed on the brakes, got out of the car and ran to the back. Runt lay there wailing. on my gosh, jimmy yelled. Are you. okay?"

Runt slowly made it to his feet. "I'm okay," he said quietly. "Are you okay?"

Jimmy said he was fine. His wife Donna joined the scene.

Runt didn't waste any time. "I hate to do this," he said, "but I need your wallet."

Jimmy Rosenberg laughed. "You want what?" he asked. "Did you say my wallet?"

"Yes," Runt answered. "This is a robbery. I need your wallet."

Suddenly, Jimmy Rosenberg lunged at Runt. He went straight for the throat.

Both men went to the ground. Donna Rosenberg took her purse and tried to slam it over Runt's head. Unfortunately, she only hit her husband.

Runt was a great athlete, and he easily got away. The big glasses he was wearing fell off his head and bounced on the ground. Runt knew he had to retrieve them. His fingerprints would be all over them.

As he reached down to get them, Jimmy Rosenberg tackled him again.

However, Runt twisted him around and had him in a headlock in nothing flat.

Donna Rosenberg screamed as Runt let Jimmy go.

"I'm sorry I bothered you,"

Runt yelled to the both of them as he scampered away. "I didn't mean any harm."

# CHAPTER THIRTY - SIX

Everybody in town wondered why Tom Wayne Rhyner and his dad had gone into the banking business. Tom Wayne's father, Earl, had made a ton of money selling cars.

It always seemed like they were the richest family in town, though nobody knew for sure.

The Olathe City Bank, as it was called, started small. At first, Tom Wayne and Earl focused on service for their customers who had carried over from the old owner. Their plan was to play it smart and not rock the boat early on in their ownership. They were Leary about getting into more than they could handle. After all, they had to learn the business.

However, Tom Wayne Rhyner was not a patient man. It only took a few months for him to talk Earl into taking a few chances. Tom Wayne had been watching TV and reading the newspapers. One of the reasons he was interested in banking was to use it as a way to take over businesses in the area.

One of the first businesses he would target would be Derryberry Oil and Gas.

Tom Wayne was careful when he explained his plan to Earl. It was not about the bitterness and contempt that he had for me, Runt and Mule.

He insisted that it was all business, nothing personal. Earl was no fool, though. He knew about the rivalry, so he decided to ask about it.

"Why are you so interested in taking over Clinton Derryberry?" he asked. "Do you have something personal against him?"

Tom Wayne explained things quickly.

"I don't hold grudges," he answered.

"You know that, Pop! I'm trying to get Mule Archer to do some work for me right now."

Earl wasn't so sure. "Listen, Son," he answered, "I think we can make some serious money using this bank.

I just want to make sure we don't run into trouble. If you mix business and personal feelings, you usually get burned."

Tom Wayne was ready to explain.

"We can buy out all of the old man's equipment and contracts easily," he said. "The oil field is getting ready to go again. We can be in a great position."

"What about their workforce?" Earl asked. "How much manpower do they have?"

Tom Wayne was quick with an answer.

"Well, the old man only works now to have something to do. He loves the three guys who he raised as his own kids. One of 'em, Kid Lewis, runs the daily operation. I can control him."

"What business do you have with Mule Archer?" Earl asked.

Tom Wayne was quick with an answer.

"Security," he said. "We own a bank now. We are gonna need to protect it.

There's nobody around here who is tougher than him."

Tom Wayne and Earl went on to discussing some other businesses they were interested in buying. They agreed to think about things for a while before they acted.

Earl was impressed with his son. He seemed to know what he was talking about. It was true that the Rhyner's had money. However, it was also true that they needed more money to get to where they really wanted to be financially. It was expensive to be the big shot in town all the time.

A couple of weeks went by before Earl and Tom Wayne discussed the issue again. This time Earl led the conversation.

"I like your idea," he said. "But we need to start small and go slow. The Derryberry Oil and Gas move makes the most sense."

Earl's comments were music to Tom Wayne's ears. "I agree," he answered.

"We just need to get all the ducks in a row and do it!"

"What do you think is a fair offer?" Earl asked.

"Well," Tom Wayne pondered. "I wasn't thinking about making him a fair offer."

Earl Rhyner smiled. "You have learned well, my son," he responded.

"Let me rephrase it," Earl said. "What is the starting figure that we offer Clinton Derryberry?"

Tom Wayne walked over to his father and whispered into his ear. There was nobody else in the room to hear what he said. He just felt it was best not to take any chances.

Earl leaned back in his chair and pondered the opportunity before offering a comment. "What do we do when the old man doesn't take our offer?" he asked.

Tom Wayne stared back at his father.

He hesitated before he answered

Finally, he spoke. "Then we offer more!"

# CHAPTER THIRTY – SEVEN

The following Sunday morning, Clinton Derryberry and his wife got up and prepared to go to church. They were hoping "the boys" might show up and join them, but they didn't have high hopes. It had been months since Runt, Mule or Kid had attended.

Mr. Derryberry drank almost an entire pot of coffee before he was ready to shower and get dressed. Mrs. Derryberry had been ready to go for almost two hours.

Mr. and Mrs. Derryberry had aged gracefully, but time was beginning to show. Clinton didn't look well at all. His stomach was bulging from eating too much food and drinking too much beer.

His legs were getting wobbly, and his hair was almost all gone.

He wasn't feeling well, either. He thought the coffee would get him going, but it didn't seem to work. As he sat down in the bedroom chair to put on his shoes, he felt a sharp pain in his left shoulder. His pride told him to tough it out like he had always done. His common sense told him to get his wife's attention.

However, it was too late. Clinton Derryberry slumped over and fell to the floor. There was a small thud that was barely audible, but Gladys Derryberry had ears like a rabbit. Immediately, she was in the bedroom.

There was a phone next to her side of the bed. Immediately, she called 911. She rolled Clinton over and started administering CPR. She had learned how to perform the skill at her Wednesday night church lady meeting.

Before you knew it, the two of them were in the ambulance and on the way to the hospital. Clinton barely made it. Gladys had saved his life.

On the way to the hospital, the two lovebirds stared at each other. They had never had children, though they had tried. There was no doubt it was the most disappointing thing in either of their lives. When Kid, Mule and Runt went to work for them the best days of their lives began. Though the boys were not their blood, it didn't matter. Clinton and Gladys Derryberry loved them just the same.

"Remember when Runt got his teeth knocked out?" Clinton whispered to Gladys.

Both of them giggled. "Oh yes, I do," Gladys answered. "I'll never forget it." A few seconds passed before Gladys kept the conversation going. "The funniest thing ever was when Runt threw that rock that hit me in the butt!" They both started snickering. It was important that Gladys kept talking. "I was mad as a hornet, but inside I was laughing so hard. It was all I could do to keep a straight face."

Clinton's facial expression settled. "So many memories," he whispered. "I love those boys."

"I know. I know," Gladys responded, "I love them, too. We're so lucky to have them."

"They'll take care of you, Gladys," he said quietly. "You'll be fine"

Gladys Derryberry didn't want to hear talk like that. "Hush, Clinton," she said.

"You are going to be fine. Just relax." She held his hand as tight as she could.

Clinton Derryberry closed his eyes and went to sleep. That would be the last time Gladys would ever get to talk to him. He passed a few hours later in the hospital.

The funeral was a heartbreaker.

Usually, things don't get so emotional over an old farmer, but Clinton Derryberry had a ton of friends. He was always kind to everyone, and he never met a stranger.

All three of us spoke. Runt told stories about Mr. Derryberry's life lessons. He quoted 'em all. It was hilarious. Mule talked about how he worried about us all the time. I told the whole story about how Mr. Derryberry recruited us to work for him, how the business developed and what a great example he was for us.

After the funeral, we had a feast back at the church. People stayed until after dark visiting. When the last guest finally walked out the door only four people remained in the room. It was just Me, Runt, Mule and Mrs. Derryberry. We just sat there and looked at each other.

I never felt sorrier for anyone more in my life than I did that evening for Mrs. Derryberry. Her heart was broken, and I know she felt all alone.

I tried to get some conversation going.

It led to Runt telling a few stories. Mule chimed in the best he could, but he was never much for talking.

Mrs. Derryberry started crying right in the middle of all that. She told us how much Mr. Derryberry loved us and how we were family to them. After that, she loosened up a little. Before you knew it, she was telling stories again and laughing.

Then out of the blue, she surprised us.

Right in the middle of a good story she stopped and changed directions.

"There is one thing we never understood about you boys," she said. "I know Clinton always wanted to know the truth, but he never asked."

It got kinda quiet. None of us knew what the heck she meant.

"What are you talking about?" I asked.

Mrs. Derryberry looked straight at Runt. Then she looked at Mule. Then she looked at me.

"I really want to know," she said.

"What really happened to you boys out at the old Johnson County Bridge?"

# CHAPTER THIRTY - EIGHT

It was time to take another shot at getting the pickup and the trailer full of cattle across the bridge. Mule assumed his position out in front.

He was holding the tow rope with both hands and was determined this time to get the job done.

Once again, I was the driver. There was no question that I was scared to death.

However, I couldn't show my cowardice towards Runt and Mule any longer.

My pride was on the line. I had more experience driving than any of the three of us. The problem was that even though I had the most experience, I was very unprepared to drive that truck pulling a trailer full of cattle across that long, rocking bridge with no side-rails.

Runt took his spot behind the trailer.

He was to push as hard as he could and try to keep things steady.

"Let's get this show on the road!" he hollered. "I ain't got all day!"

I put the truck in neutral and took a deep breath. I'll never forget the intensity of the moment. I looked out the windshield at Mule. He was trying to maneuver his body to where he could walk forward. He had wrapped the tow rope around his shoulders.

"I'm ready!" he screamed. "Let's go!"

Mule started walking. It took all the strength he had to take just one step.

Runt was pushing from the back of the trailer as hard as he could push. We barely moved.

The truck rocked back and forth as Mule collected his energy and made a series of pulls. Finally, the momentum started and slowly we creaked forward at a ridiculously slow pace.

After ten minutes, Mule had to take a break. He was exhausted. We had moved about twenty feet. It never occurred to us that sitting still on the bridge was not a smart move.

Nobody said anything while Mule rested. Only the cattle talked. They mooed and hissed. I could sense that they were terrified, too.

Finally, Mule got up and started to pull again. We seemed to get started easier this time. Actually, we were moving a little. Things were looking up.

What happened next still causes my stomach to sink down to my knees.

I have to close my eyes when I think about it.

I don't know how Mule slipped. It just happened. Maybe the bottom of his boots went out from under him, or maybe the tow rope got away from him.

I don't know. We've never discussed it.

When he slipped, the momentum of the surge stopped. The truck jerked backwards. Runt was caught back there.

Somehow, he slid underneath the cattle trailer and got away.

All I knew to do was to slam on the brakes. That's when the trailer slid off the tracks. I looked in the rear-view mirror. I swear the left rear tire of the trailer was sitting on the corner of the bridge.

Everything came to a stop. I looked back up in front to check on Mule, but he wasn't there. He had disappeared.

I crawled to the passenger side door.

There was no way I could get out of the driver's side. I would fall right into the river.

Carefully, I slipped out of the truck.

"Mule!" I screamed. "Where are you?"

There was no answer. "Mule!" I yelled again. "Where are you?"

I got on all fours and crawled to the side of the bridge. I looked down. Mule was hanging off the bridge. We had lynched him. The tow rope was around his neck, and he was struggling to get loose.

I didn't know what to do. I looked back at the truck. That was when I saw Runt trying to get the tow rope off the front bumper. His effort was in vain, though.

Superman couldn't have got it loose. I could tell he was really frustrated. The cattle were making so much noise that it was hard to think. All of a sudden, Runt stopped dealing with the rope, and he ran back to the trailer.

He screamed at the cattle.

"Shut Up!" It seemed like he knew them personally.

What happened next was simply amazing. Runt quickly made his way back to the front of the truck. He took off his shoes. Before I knew it, he was climbing down the tow rope to Mule.

When he did, I guess it relieved the tension. All of a sudden, Mule seemed to start making some progress on getting out of the hangman's noose. However, he couldn't quite get out of trouble. His face looked like it was on fire.

Runt got down low enough to stick his right foot right into Mule's neck.

"Stick my foot in the loop!" he yelled.

There was all kinds of wobbling and squirming and heaving, but somehow Runt got his foot in there. Before you knew it, Mule Archer slipped out of the tow rope and fell into the Kansas River. The splash was as clean as a professional diver.

Suddenly, Runt released his grip and fell into the river himself. He hit the water feet first making a beautiful entrance.

It took a few minutes before the both of them came up out of the water together. I don't know how Runt found him and pulled him out of there. We've never talked about it. I just know they came up at the same time. Before I knew it, they were both sitting on the bank of the river. They were safe.

I watched the whole thing from the bridge. The pickup finally stopped rocking, and the trailer sat perfectly still. I couldn't believe what I had just seen! Even crazier than that, those cattle were so quiet, you would think that they were asleep.

# CHAPTER THIRTY - NINE

Tom Wayne Rhyner and his dad, Earl, were busy building their business empire. Tom Wayne had plenty of distractions, though. He was now engaged to Runt's ex-wife, Macy, and they were planning a big wedding. He was also going to legally adopt Runt's daughter, Georgia.

But a funny thing occurred one night at dinner. As she was eating her steak, Macy started talking about Runt in a positive tone. That stunned Tom Wayne. He had never heard her say much good about her ex-husband.

Most of her comments had been very negative.

"I have to admit," she said. "He's really a sweetheart. I loved him so much.

We just couldn't make it. For all his good qualities, Runt just couldn't get it together. He was always kind of a vagabond when it came to work." Of course, that made Tom Wayne furious, but he was careful to hide it. He hated Runt Suggs more than anything or anybody in the world. His master plan as the new bank president was to find a way to take over Derryberry Oil and Gas. After that, he would fire me and Runt. He never let on to Macy or his dad about his plan, but they always had an idea of what he was doing. There was never much trust when it came to Tom Wayne.

"I thought you despised him," Tom Wayne asked Macy.

She looked at him and smiled. "I did despise him," she answered. "But it's tough going through a divorce with someone. Surely, you understand that.

Lord knows, you have been married enough times. It brings out the worst in you."

Tom Wayne acted like he understood, but he was about to explode on the inside. His jealousy intensified. Macy had no idea that she had just opened a giant can of worms.

"He is so good to Georgia," she continued. "My mom always noticed how caring he was with her. I have to give him some credit."

That last comment burned Tom Wayne to the bone. "Let's change the subject," he said. "I don't want to talk about him anymore. We need to get out of here!"

He got up and left the table. Macy was still eating her dinner.

The next morning, Tom Wayne started working on a proposition to offer Mrs. Derryberry. He wanted to purchase Derryberry Oil and Gas right now. He had been studying all the information that he had available. His data was limited, but he did notice some things that helped. Clinton Derryberry only borrowed money to help his credit score, and he quickly paid it back. There was no debt. After all, the company mainly did manual labor jobs. There was not a need for a lot of equipment.

There were some small accounting problems, but the thing Tom Wayne was looking for was not in the records.

There was no trace of any payment either through the Derryberry's personal account or through the business account to Runt Suggs for anything other than labor.

Runt had always told Macy that he had connections to "old money." She just took it for granted that meant the money came from Mr. and Mrs. Derryberry. However, there were no records of that.

"This doesn't add up," Tom Wayne thought to himself. "Surely, he didn't give Runt cash. Or did he?"

Tom Wayne thought about it all night.

"How did Runt get all that money?" He couldn't get his mind off the subject. The next morning while eating breakfast, he thought of a plan.

"If Mule won't spy on Runt, then I will just get someone else to do it," he thought. "I have to find out where he is getting all that money."

Tom Wayne really didn't have a lot during the day that he just had to do.

That was the life he lived. It had always been like that. He did whatever he wanted. Not many people had ever lived such a sheltered existence as him. He knew no other way but to be the Big Shot.

He made his way over to the Highway Patrol office. It only took him a few minutes to find out where Mule's desk was located. Tom Wayne didn't care about any protocol when approaching a law officer. He just walked right in the door and said he was there to speak with Mule Archer.

Mule was talking on the phone with another Trooper down in Franklin County. Tom Wayne started knocking on the window of his door. The bang, bang, bang noise startled Mule. He started trying to end his conversation with the other officer. Bang, Bang, Bang!

Tom Wayne rapped his knuckles on the window again. He lashed out at Mule like he was already his employer. "Can I count on you to honor your commitment or not?"

Mule was cool about the whole meeting. He had learned how to deal with arrogant people. "I've never made any commitment to you," he answered.

He lashed out at Mule like he was already his employer. "Can I count on you to honor your commitment or not?"

Mule was cool about the whole meeting. He had learned how to deal with arrogant people. "I've never made any commitment to you," he answered.

"Yes, you did," Tom Wayne said sarcastically. "You are going to follow your buddy, Runt, around for a few days to see where he is getting all this money."

Mule sat down behind his desk. "I made no such commitment," he said.

"I don't see any reason to follow him around. He hasn't committed any crime that I know of, Sir."

That didn't slow Tom Wayne down at all. "Just follow him on Friday and Saturday nights for a couple of weeks.

I'll pay you $50 an hour, ten hours maximum per weekend. That's $500 a weekend, Mule. Think about it."

Mule was human. Five hundred dollars for a few hours on a weekend was a heck of a side job. The temptation was a little overwhelming. The fact that Mule didn't respond gave Tom Wayne the answer he wanted. He knew he had almost lured Mule into his trap.

Mule stood up and looked out the door. He was in quite an odd position.

Five hundred dollars a weekend could save his marriage. However, he would be turning against his best friend. The voices in his head weren't just talking.

They were screaming both sides of the argument.

Finally, Mule turned to face Tom Wayne. "What if I don't find out anything bad about him?" he asked.

"Maybe he is just good with his money."

Tom Wayne Rhyner got up out of his chair. He put the cup of coffee right in the middle of Mule's desk. The two men locked eyes.

"He's doing something for that money," Tom Wayne said. "Now listen to me. I am paying you good money to find out what it is. Monday morning, I want a full report."

# CHAPTER FORTY

Saturday afternoon rolled around. Mule was in such a bad mood he couldn't even talk to his wife.

He felt like he had made a deal with the devil. His closet was a mess. There were hats, boots, and clothes all over the place. He knew he had to use some type of cover that Runt wouldn't recognize.

It would be a longshot that he would be spotted, but he knew he had to be careful. Though he had never set the world on fire professionally, Runt was very smart.

It wasn't hard to find him. Mule simply made his way over to the apartment where Runt lived and kept his distance.

His white, unmarked car fit nicely into the parking lot. Mule sat there for an hour before Runt walked down the steps of his second-floor residence.

Quickly, he was in his pickup, and he was gone.

Mule Archer was no James Bond. There had been some duty of following people that involved him in the past, but he was never the lead honcho. in fact, he felt like quite an amateur. That was why he gave Runt a long leash.

"Maybe I'll lose him," Mule thought to himself. "Then I'll be off the hook." It turned out that Runt was in no hurry, though. He hit the off ramp and jumped on the highway heading to Kansas City. Mule followed several cars behind. He thought that he really had lost him when Runt exited the freeway and parked his truck. If not for a stroke of luck, the night would have been over for Mule. However, he picked the correct exit ramp. When he turned right, he caught a glimpse of Runt's truck out of his right eye.

Suddenly, a bus pulled out of the parking lot. Mule decided to follow it.

He didn't know if Runt was on board or not. The trip to Kansas City was about 30 miles. It was getting dark. Mule felt guilty, but he also knew he was making better wages working for Tom Wayne Rhyner than any other job he had ever had.

The bus stopped in downtown Kansas City. Mule parked up the road a bit where he could see the folks getting off the bus. The very last person to step down was Runt Suggs. Mule smiled to himself. Maybe he was good at this kind of work after all.

Kult started walking north. I his is gonna be tough," Mule thought. "I wish he was in his truck. That's a lot easier to follow."

Before he knew it, Runt was at his destination, the Hendrickson House.

There was a big poker game going on in the back room there tonight.

Mule peered in to see, but there was no way he could tell what the heck was going on. He was going to have to get out of the car and get closer, so that was what he did.

He slipped behind the corner of a building. From this angle, it was virtually impossible for Runt to see him. Mule didn't smoke, but he acted like he was enjoying a cigarette. That way he would look natural.

"Next week I need to bring some smokes," he said to himself.

Mule leaned around the corner to get a good view. "He looks like he is hiding, too," he thought. "What the heck is going on here?"

Both of them stood at a corner behind a building for the next thirty minutes.

Neither of them moved. Runt had no idea his best friend was lurking across the street behind a corner. He had found his victim and was ready for his approach. Suddenly, he stepped away from the building and started walking.

Mule wasn't sure what to do. He stepped around the corner and started following Runt. Suddenly, out of the blue, a man approached him.

"Hey!" the man said. "You're the Midnight Rider! Yeah, that's you, isn't it? I saw your picture in the papers, the Midnight Rider."

Mule was taken aback. Runt just kept on walking. The man continued with his questions. "Can I take my picture with you?" he asked. "I can't believe it, the Midnight Rider!"

"I'm sorry, Sir," Mule answered. "You must be mistaken."

The man continued to badger Mule.

"I know it's you," he said. "Come on, let's take a picture. My wife will never believe it."

Mule knew he had to turn and walk away from Runt. He was getting too close, so off he went. He couldn't walk fast enough.

Meanwhile, Runt was zeroed in on making his first robbery of the night just thirty yards away.

The man started screaming at Mule.

"Hey, Midnight Rider! To heck with you!

You're a fraud!"

"The Midnight Rider" was all that Runt heard. He looked down towards the man who was yelling and watched a broad-shouldered guy walking away.

Runt was just about to approach his mark, but he stopped. It was too big a risk. He turned and started walking the other way. "The Midnight Rider," he thought to himself. "I can't believe it!"

# CHAPTER FORTY - ONE

On the following Tuesday, I got a phone call from Runt. "Kid," he said, "what are you doing Saturday night? Let's go out on the town."

I didn't get very many invitations to do much of anything, so I jumped at the chance. "Sure," I answered. "What do you want to do?"

"Well," Runt said, "I know this place in Kansas City called The Dancing Bear. I bet you'll like it. It's on Magnolia Street.

I'll meet you there at 9:00."

I didn't ask any questions. I just said I would be there. It would be great to hang out with him on a Saturday night.

The weekend rolled around. Runt slept in Saturday morning like he always did.

He watched some TV and ate an early dinner. Soon, it was time to go to Kansas City.

Mule was parked down the street. He knew he had to be more careful this week than last.

Runt left his apartment at 6:30 p.m. and started his normal routine. He parked his truck at the bus stop and hopped on board with about thirty people. The trip took about an hour.

Soon, he was walking to a shopping mall close to downtown. For some reason, he talked to an old man in a wheelchair for a long time.

Pretty soon, it was time to head to The Dancing Bear. Runt loved to walk, and it was a nice night. Though it was about four miles to the club, he enjoyed the exercise.

The Dancing Bear was in the seediest part of Kansas City. I did my best just to find a place to park my truck where it wouldn't get stolen. I remember thinking, "What is Runt doing hanging out in a place like this. He's really hit rock bottom."

I didn't give it much more thought than that. I walked up to the door. A beggar hit me up for money when I got there.

"I'm sorry," I said. "I have to go into the club."

As soon as I walked in the door, some guy yelled at me. "Hey," he said. "What's your name?"

"My name is Hayden Lewis," I answered. "My friends call me Kid."

The man looked at a piece of paper before he spoke. "Yeah," he said, "I figured that was you. We have a place reserved for you up in the balcony.

Come on, follow me. I'll take you up there."

I never get preferential treatment anywhere, so I followed him upstairs.

The man opened a set of drapes to his left. Inside, there was a table and some chairs. The balcony had a great view of the stage down below.

I sat down. "How do I get a beer?" I asked.

"Coming right up," the man answered.

"You drink Coors Light, don't you?"

"Yeah," I answered. "I drink Coors Light. How did you know that?" He didn't answer.

I sat down and enjoyed the show. A waiter with a fresh brew was there in an instant. I felt like I was in tall cotton. A guy down on the stage started playing a guitar and singing a song. I stayed there and just relaxed. It felt pretty good.

The drapes were closed. I had my own private box. I put my feet up on the rail and leaned back.

Runt arrived at the scene, but he decided to go into a bar down the street.

He never made it to The Dancing Bear.

It was pushing nine o'clock. That was when the skirmish started in the club down below me. It was really nothing, just a couple of guys arguing with each other. They both stood up and yelled a little bit, but there was no physical confrontation.

What I didn't know was that some guy took off out the front door. He knew that an unmarked police car was parked two streets down. The car was a white Ford Crown

Victoria. The man ran right up to the car and started tapping on the window with his hand.

Mule Archer cracked his window.

"I know you're a cop," the man said.

"There is a big fight going on in The Dancing Bear. We need your help, right now!"

Mule was stunned that his identity had been made that easily. Now, he was in quite a dilemma. It was his duty to act when called upon. However, the last thing he wanted to do was to go into The Dancing Bear.

But in his mind, he had no choice. He had to go. It was his responsibility to respond. He followed the man right up to the front door. As soon as he entered, the bouncer saw him.

"Over here!" he yelled. "Two guys are getting ready to fight! I think one of them is armed! Follow me!"

Mule followed the bouncer upstairs.

They came to a small room that had drapes for an entrance. Mule looked at the drapes. When he turned around, he noticed that he was all alone. The bouncer had left the scene.

Mule took out mis gun. slowly, he reached for the curtains. With one swift movement, he raised his weapon with his right hand and yanked the curtains away with his left hand.

I was sitting in a chair with my feet up on the rail drinking a beer. When I saw Mule pointing a loaded weapon at me, I almost had a heart attack.

"How ya doin', Mule?" I quivered. "Do you think you could point that gun in another direction?"

# CHAPTER FORTY - TWO

Mule and I had A good heart to heart conversation, but he never admitted that he was following Runt. He claimed that he was following someone else, and the whole thing was a big coincidence.

Of course, Mule was a terrible liar, and I knew something was up. I was always pretty gullible, but I never considered myself stupid.

The next afternoon, I called Runt at his apartment. "You never showed!" I said it with some venom. "What's going on?" Runt was very calm. "Yes, I did show, Sir!" he responded. "I waited for two hours. I thought you were mad at me or something."

"I went to The Dancing Bear," I answered. "That was where you told me to go."

"The Dancing Bear?" Runt asked. "I said to meet me at the place next door to the Dancing Bear, a place called Mandatory Training."

"Don't pull my chain, Runt!" I answered. "You told me to meet you at The Dancing Bear!"

Runt wouldn't give an inch. He got mad, and we ended the conversation.

That just confused me even more. I didn't even mention that Mule showed up. I didn't speak to Runt or Mule for almost two months after that.

Tom Wayne Rhyner and Macy Suggs' wedding date was rapidly approaching.

I didn't get an invitation. That was okay, though. I didn't want to go. However, Runt and Mule were invited. It was Tom Wayne's idea. He wanted to stick the needle into their sides a little deeper and cause more trouble between us.

However, that was the subject that broke the ice and got the three of us back together. Runt asked us if it was improper for him to decline the invitation. I thought he should go, but Mule said he shouldn't.

"You should go for your daughter's sake," I said.

"That's why I don't think I should go," Runt responded. "I might do something stupid."

After hearing that response, I agreed.

By committee, we decided that Runt should politely skip the wedding. He sent an expensive clock as a gift, one that he knew Macy had always wanted. The big night was on the following Saturday. The wedding was slated to start at 7:00 p.m. sharp. By then, Runt was already in Oklahoma City.

He had caught a bus earlier in the day.

Somehow, he had learned about a big poker game going on over on the west side of town.

Runt used the same plan that he had used many times before in Kansas City.

He adjusted his teeth and his eye. He hadn't shaved all week and hadn't cut his hair in a month. The dark clothes that he wore made it hard to see him.

He made his way to a building on 73rd Street and set up in a parking lot. A black Cadillac pulled up to the building.

The first victim was a man about the age of fifty. It was obvious that he was going to the card game. He was all by himself, so Runt approached him as he closed his car door.

"Sir," Runt started, "did you know you have a headlight out?"

The man seemed a little startled. "No," he answered. "I didn't know that."

"Yes, Sir," Runt continued. "This one right over here on the left front is burned out."

Runt walked right over to it. The man followed him.

"Well, thanks," the victim said quietly.

Runt went in to close the deal. "Sir," he said sternly. "I need your wallet. This is a hold up."

The man looked at Runt and started laughing. "No, it isn't," he answered.

"I'm not giving you anything.

"However, Runt was way ahead of him.

He pulled out the gun and held it down at his side. "I need your wallet," Runt said. "This isn't a joke. Please, Sir, just cooperate. I don't want anyone to get hurt."

The man pulled out his wallet and handed it to Runt. It was easy. At least that was what Runt thought. Suddenly though, the man lunged at Runt and tried to tackle him. They went to the ground. Runt was much younger and stronger. A five-minute skirmish turned into an all-out fight for survival.

Runt finally took the gun and hit the man on the side of the head. The man sank onto his back. Runt got up and took off into the darkness. He walked a good two miles, maybe three.

He spotted a gas station up ahead.

Luckily, the bathroom was unlocked, so Runt slipped in and locked the door behind him. He flipped on the lights and looked in the mirror. That was when he first saw all the blood.

Not knowing where it was coming from, he took off his coat and shirt. The cut was from the top of his chest down through the side of his abdomen. He was bleeding profusely. The man in the Cadillac had cut him with a knife.

# CHAPTER FORTY - THREE

My job as the head of Derryberry Oil and Gas had become pretty mundane. I sat in an office all day and answered the phone. We had a lady in place to do all the work, and she did a very good job. It was a pretty good deal. Every now and then, I would venture out into the field to see what was going on out there. It was always great to get out of the office.

One day I got a phone call from one of our most loyal customers. Dixon Brothers Oil owned a lot of rigs in the area and called on us often. The roustabout business included almost any kind of work. Derryberry Oil and Gas executed everything from running water hose line to examining pipe thread. We did pretty much anything needed.

The foreman at a Dixon Brothers rig had a complaint about some work we were doing. He wanted me to come out and have a meeting. I got in my pickup and headed out to the site. It was about thirty miles away.

After I arrived, it took me a little while to find the tool pusher. He was over by the reserve pit looking at something. I didn't notice that anything was out of the ordinary.

I walked up to him and started a conversation. "How are you doing, Sir?" I asked. "I'm Kid Lewis from Derryberry Oil and Gas. I understand that you wanted to meet with me."

The tool pusher wasn't interested in talking to me. "I don't need to meet with you," he said. "Some other guy told me to call you and set up a meeting."

"That's odd," I thought. "Who is this other guy?" I asked.

The tool pusher was busy doing whatever he was doing. "I don't know where he is," he responded. "I just did what I was told to do. I set up a meeting."

I looked around to see if there was someone on the site who was available to help me, but I couldn't find anybody.

I really didn't think the situation was that big of a deal. I bumped around the rig for a while looking for something or somebody that needed my attention. I found nothing and no one.

I was ready to give up and go back to the office, so I got in my pickup and headed for the exit of the site.

That was when I noticed a big Ford pickup truck barreling down the gravel road towards the rig. Dust, rocks and debris blew way up into the air behind it. There was no place else for the truck to go. I figured it was heading to where I was parked, so I waited.

Into the site came the big truck. After it turned into the gate, it crept toward my pickup. When it got to within about ten feet, it stopped.

It was a gloomy day; the skies were cloudy and the wind was blowing like always. It looked like it was going to rain. I still couldn't figure out who wanted to talk to me.

Suddenly, the door of the big pickup truck opened and a man jumped out.

I recognized him immediately. It was Tom Wayne Rhyner.

He didn't say anything at first. He just looked at me like I was as welcome as an outhouse breeze.

Tom Wayne was wearing a black felt cowboy hat. He was a big guy, and he looked a little imposing. It made me think back to the days when I was scared to death of him.

Without saying a word, he pulled out a piece of paper from his back pocket. I watched him unfold it. There were no pleasantries exchanged.

"This is a legal document," Tom Wayne said. "I bought Derryberry Oil and Gas from Mrs. Derryberry. I no longer need you as an employee. There will be no severance pay. You are not to go back to the office. If you do, I will file a trespassing charge against you.

All your valuables will be boxed up by a third party and dropped off at your home this afternoon."

That was it. Tom Wayne Rhyner folded the paper and handed it to me. He got back into his pickup and turned around.

As he drove away, he hit the accelerator with a little extra juice to make sure he stirred up a good dirt storm. He knew it would blow right into my face.

# CHAPTER FORTY - FOUR

Tom Wayne Rhyner droves straight from that rig site to a highway that headed to Johnson County. He had done his research, and he knew exactly where Runt would be working that day. He drove up in his big pickup truck and parked on the side of the road.

Runt was watching some work done by a grader and didn't see him. Tom Wayne walked up to a county worker and demanded to see the supervisor.

After all, he was Tom Wayne Rhyner.

He was the owner of a bank in Olathe, Kansas. The supervisor he wanted to talk to was Runt Suggs.

The county worker got Runt's attention and told him he was being summoned. When Runt left the grader, he saw Tom Wayne.

"How was the wedding?" Runt asked politely. He was still very sore from the wound he had suffered only a couple of weeks ago. He didn't need and wasn't in the mood for any trouble with anyone.

However, Tom Wayne was in the mood for trouble.

"I have something to show you." Tom Wayne said it with a smile on his face.

Runt was enraged at the sight of Tom Wayne. He couldn't stand to be in the same room with him much less being forced to carry on a conversation.

The tone of the meeting changed.

"What do you want?" Runt asked.

"I just wanted to show you something," Tom Wayne answered.

"Mule has been working for me."

Runt didn't really comprehend what it all meant. "So," he said. "That's none of my business."

Tom Wayne pulled a piece of paper out of his pocket and handed it to Runt.

Sure enough, it was a copy of a $500 check made out to Riley Archer.

"Here are some more," Tom Wayne said. "I want you to see them."

Tom Wayne handed Runt a small stack of papers. All had copies of checks made out to Mule. Each check was for $500.

"I hired Mule to watch you, Runt," he said. "I didn't trust you, never have.

Mule agreed to follow you to find out where you were getting all this extra money. Of course, he didn't find out any information. I'm not surprised. I just wanted you to know that he turned on you like a snake."

Tom Wayne got back in his pickup and drove away. His mission was complete.

In the course of an hour, he had obtained his objectives. He had fired me from the only job I ever had. I was out of work for the first time in my life. He had informed Runt that his best friend had betrayed him. He was sure that would ruin their relationship forever. He knew that he didn't have to do anything to Mule. Word would get back to him very soon that Runt knew he had taken money to follow his best friend. Tom Wayne droves back to the bank. He Had settled an old score against three guys that he had hated for years. He had married the wife of one of his rivals. Of course, his plan had been in place for a long, long time.

# CHAPTER FORTY - FIVE

"Tom Wayne Rhyner told me that your job would be secure forever," Mrs. Derryberry said with fierce emotion.

"I can't believe this! I just can't believe this!"

However, it was true. Tom Wayne, his dad Earl, and their bank had bought Derryberry Oil and Gas. "Did you have a witness with you?" I asked Mrs. Derryberry. "Was there anybody else there?"

Mrs. Derryberry dropped her head into her hands. "No," she said quietly. "It was just me and Tom Wayne."

I let her cry for a while. I didn't know what else to do.

"I had to have the money," she said. "I just had to have the money. He told me nothing would change with you, Kid." It didn't surprise me that Tom Wayne had lied to her. He was a no count scoundrel if there ever was one. It hurt so bad. I had worked for the company for over twenty years. Now I was out of a job and had nowhere to go.

"It's okay," I said. "I'll find something else to do. You never know. It could have been a blessing."

I left the house while Mrs. Derryberry was still crying. When I got home, all my belongings were sitting in front of the door. At least, Tom Wayne did what he said he would do about that.

A few hours later there was a knock on the door. It was Runt. He showed up with a half case of beer. We talked and talked and talked, but we didn't come up with any solutions. Tom Wayne had won this round for sure.

"Why are we still in a pissing match with him, Runt?" I asked. "I mean, isn't this feud pretty silly?"

Runt looked at me like I was crazy.

"Feud," he said. "I thought it was a war!"

He got up and started walking around the living room. "I've always hated him," he said. "Always!"

Runt picked up his pace as he walked around the room. "He's the biggest bully ever! I knew he would go after

Macy when we divorced. She's the best-looking woman in town. I don't think he really loves her. He just knows how bad it hurts me."

It got quiet for a while before he started talking again. "He's married my ex-wife, fired you and caused Mule to turn on me. He's three for three." I didn't know what to say. Between the stress and the beer, I was really tired. I just wanted to go to bed.

"Maybe," I thought, "this is just a nightmare."

But it wasn't. "Runt," I said. "You can sleep on the couch if you have drunk too much to drive, but I'm going to bed. I ain't up to no more worrying about Tom Wayne Rhyner tonight. I'm exhausted."

I did what I said. However, Runt stayed in the living room. He was drinking beer and watching TV. The next morning when I got up, he was gone. I made some coffee and stirred around a little bit. Finally, I sat down and started watching The Today Show.

I glanced at the coffee table and saw something odd. There was some money sticking out of a folded Sports Illustrated magazine. Slowly, I opened it. There lay three $100 bills.

# CHAPTER FORTY - SIX

Mule Archer was fighting some serious demons. He hadn't spoken to Runt in almost three months, but he had bigger problems than repairing trust with one of his best friends. Right now, he was busy working on repairing his marriage.

Things had gone bad with his wife, Laura. There was never enough money.

Not even the $500 per week in cash that Tom Wayne was paying him helped that much. Laura found a way to spend it as fast as she got it.

However, Little Gary held Mule and Laura together. The county fair was in session, and that was always one of the highlights of the year. Little Gary loved the carnival atmosphere, and he really loved the rides. He was twelve years old.

Mule bought a ticket and put Little Gary on the Tilt-o-Whirl. It was his favorite ride. As soon as it wound up, Laura started in on Mule.

"How are we going to send him to college?" she asked. "We have no savings. How are we going to do it, Mule? We owe it to him."

Mule was just trying to enjoy the evening. He didn't really have much of an answer.

"Well," he said, "maybe he will get a football scholarship."

That comment really put Laura into a bad mood. She turned around and walked away.

After riding a few rides Mule, Laura and Little Gary made their way over to the games. Mule, Runt and I grew up throwing darts in bars, so it was just natural for Mule to want to teach his son how he used to school us.

"You take the dart and put it right even with your right eyeball," he lectured.

"Only bring your hand back about six inches, then flick it at the target. Don't throw it."

Little Gary seemed to be a natural.

Every shot hit the board. Mule was so proud.

"Chip off the old block," he thought to himself.

However, across the way, standing at the ring toss stood a man named Eric Stonehill. He was wearing a t-shirt and blue jeans. Only thirty-five years old, he was a rock of a human being.

Stonehill had been watching Mule since he saw him enter the fairgrounds. He recognized him from the newspapers.

Mule laughed as Little Gary pitched dart after dart at the board. Suddenly, Mule stood up tall and looked around.

That was when he saw Eric Stonehill.

Their eyes locked immediately.

Mule acted like there was nothing unusual at the carnival. He went out of his way to appease both his wife and his son. A great day was had by all. Soon, it was time to go home.

The family car was parked on a gravel road by some trees down by the highway. It was late in the day, and there were no other vehicles parked in the area.

Mule, Laura and Little Gary were only about twenty feet from the van when all of a sudden, Eric Stonehill walked out from behind a tree. He stood about fifty feet from them.

It startled Laura at first, but she had seen this movie before. Without even acknowledging Mule, she grabbed Little Gary by the arm and scurried to the car.

She had the door open in a second.

"Get in the car, Gary," she said in a flux.

"Hurry, get in the car!"

Little Gary didn't cause any trouble. He did as he was told. Before you knew it, he was seat belted into the car and the door was slammed shut.

Laura jumped into the driver's seat, turned on the ignition and peeled out.

Gravel blew into Mule's face as she drove away. She never looked back.

Mule looked straight at Eric Stonehill.

"What do you want?" he asked him.

Eric Stonehill took his time before he answered. "You know what I want," he answered.

Mule straightened his back before he spoke. "I have no quarrel with you," he said.

The look on Eric Stonehill's face worried Mule. He had seen that look before. Slowly, Stonehill pulled out a huge knife and held it down by his side.

"You're the Midnight Rider, aren't you?" he asked.

Mule didn't want to answer, but after a few seconds, he had to respond. "I have been called that before," he said.

"You won't shoot at me if all I have is a knife," Eric Stonehill said loudly.

"That's right!" Mule yelled back.

Suddenly, Eric Stonehill pitched the knife on the ground. He reached behind his back with his right hand and pulled out a Colt .45. He did not point it at Mule. He held it down at his side.

Mule was in all out focus. "I don't have a gun," he said.

Eric Stonehill laughed. "You have a gun," he answered. "You might as well get it out of your belt cause I'm gonna shoot you in about two minutes."

"No, you won't," Mule yelled.

"Yes, I will," answered Eric Stonehill.

Mule knew it was time to take action. slowly, he reached behind his back and retrieved his gun.

The two men stood fifty feet apart staring at each other. Each of them held their right arms straight down at their sides. Each held a gun in their right hand.

"How we gonna do this?" Mule yelled at Eric Stonehill.

"I don't know," Stonehill answered.

"You tell me!"

"I suggest you go your way, and I go my way," Mule answered.

A few seconds transpired before Eric Stonehill spoke. "I'll tell you what," he said. "I'm going to count to ten. On ten, fire!"

Suddenly, Mule thought back to the day after he shot Johnny Radford. He remembered what Runt asked him.

"Why did you kill him? Why didn't you just shoot him in the leg?" The thought made Mule focus even more on Eric Stonehill.

"One, two, three," Eric Stonehill counted. The two men peered into each other's eyes.

"Four, five, six," he continued. "Seven, eight, nine, TEN!"

Everyone back at the fair heard it. A deathly silence fell upon the grounds.

It was obvious that a gunshot had just been fired.

# CHAPTER FORTY - SEVEN

Major t. J. Smith thought he had seen it all. He had been in the law enforcement business for thirty-three years.

However, this event topped them all. He had heard about guys like Eric Stonehill during his days as a peacekeeper, but he had never actually dealt with anyone like that.

"He was wanted in four states," Major Smith told his commanding officer.

"Murder, armed robbery and extortion, he was one of the worst of the worst." Mule Archer sat in the corner of the room and didn't say a word.

"He was looking for a fight," Major Smith continued. "He wanted to make a big name for himself. He wanted to kill Captain Archer."

Major Smith took a swig of his coffee before he shuffled his report. He had stayed up all night preparing it.

"Stonehill killed a police officer in Little Rock, and he's been on the run ever since. A month later, he beat a man to death in Shreveport outside a casino.

They identified him on both the house camera and the parking lot camera. He was accused of armed robbery three times. We just couldn't catch up to him."

None of the information made Mule feel any better. He was devastated. It had happened again. Eric Stonehill had spotted him and knew he was the Midnight Rider. Mule was the man with the big gun on his hip, the baddest dude in the territory. If you took him down, you became the big gun yourself.

That wasn't the only thing. Mule knew his marriage was over. Laura had already spoken to a lawyer. She was tired of all this, and she was serious this time. Mule's lifestyle put her and Little Gary in danger every time they left the house. It was a humiliating way of life, a way of life that she absolutely hated. Mule sat right there in the corner and made the decision. He had to let her go.

She was right about the whole thing.

It wasn't fair to her or Little Gary to live like that. When she brought up a divorce this time, he would agree without any argument.

The commander got up out of his chair and walked over to Mule. He grabbed a chair and sat down face to face with him. He really didn't know what to say, so he just got straight to the point.

"Captain", he said. "You're a fine lawman. This is a tough situation. You know that."

Major Smith sat silent for a couple of minutes before he spoke. He was thinking about what he was going to do.

First though, he had to let his boss have some quality time with Mule.

"You know the investigation will take some time," the commander said. "You will be on desk duty. I know you hate that, but you have to do it. Time will pass, and soon this will be over."

Mule couldn't get himself to look the commander in the eye. For some reason, he just couldn't do it.

"Go home and be with your family.

It will make you feel better," the commander advised.

That was when Mule started to cry. He couldn't help himself. He sobbed and sobbed and sobbed. Finally, Major Smith came over and tried to hug him. It was awkward, but Mule appreciated it. Soon, Mule pulled it together and stopped.

However, his eyes were bloodshot red, and tears ran down his face.

Major Smith thought he had really done a good job of handling the situation. However, he wasn't sure what Mule Archer's future would be with the Kansas Highway Patrol. He had never seen a lawman who was a target like the Midnight Rider.

Mule stood up and grabbed his coat.

Slowly, he made his way to the door.

Both Major Smith and the commander watched him leave.

On the way to his car Mule started thinking about his next move. He called Laura, but he knew she wouldn't answer. He drove home and entered the house, but nobody was there. An envelope sat on the kitchen table.

It took Mule two hours and six beers before he opened it. When he did, it said: "Mule, I will always love you, but I can't live like this. Not only are you dangerous to be around, but we are broke, too. I am not arguing about it this time.

I demand a divorce. You have two days to get your belongings and get out of the house. Don't try to talk me out of it. I'm serious. Laura.

Mule did as she said. He didn't have that much to pack. It only took a little while to get it all together.

"It's ironic," he thought to himself. "I'm getting kicked out of my own house when there is nobody home."

He knew where to go. It was a no-brainer. There was only one family member who would take him. He knew that. He wobbled out to his car.

"If I get pulled over, I'll get a DWI," he thought. "I've drunk way too much too drive."

Being the good law-abiding citizen that he was, he slept in his own driveway the rest of the night. The next morning, he headed to my house. He knew I would take him in without question.

He stopped by a local store to get some coffee and doughnuts.

As he stepped out of the car, he looked around. "Well," he thought. "I better check to see if somebody is here who wants to kill me."

# CHAPTER FORTY – EIGHT

Having a roommate was A pretty radical change for me. I had been living by myself for years. Mule was good, though. He mainly stayed to himself, and he didn't bother me at all. It was great to have somebody to drink beer and watch sports with for a change, and he paid for dinner almost every night.

Since I was out of a job, it was good timing for me to have him around. I needed help paying the rent now. A month after Tom Wayne Rhyner fired me, I got a job offer. One of the oil companies that Derryberry Oil and Gas serviced needed someone to represent them. They needed more places for prospective drilling.

After a few weeks, I started getting the hang of it. People seemed to warm up to me. They said I was non-threatening, and they could trust me. It wasn't a hard deal to sell when you told them you would pay them just to survey for oil on their land.

One day I went out to a couple's homeplace to talk to them about a deal. Wanda Zimmerman was the spokesperson for the family. Bill Zimmerman mainly just sat there and smoked Marlboro cigarettes. He also drank a lot of coffee.

"How do I know we can trust your big shot oiliest?" Wanda asked the question as soon as we sat down at the kitchen table. "We've been here for forty years.

All of a sudden, you tell us there might be oil here. I don't trust you." Wanda had a good point. There was no "for sure" thing. Big hopes and big dreams had been dashed many times before.

"I can't tell you there is oil on your property, Mrs. Zimmerman," I answered. "This is just a first step. We'll pay you just to allow us to come out and run some tests. We'll give you an answer as soon as we can."

Wanda wasn't sold. "How long will it take for you to tell us?" she asked.

"Well, I don't know," I said. "I'm not in charge of that. We might not even make it out here for a year."

"A year?!" Wanda all but screamed. "I don't want to wait for a year!"

"It's important to temper our expectations, Mrs. Zimmerman," I said.

"This is not an overnight thing. It's a long-term project."

Wanda reached into her pocket and pulled out a Salem Light cigarette. She didn't ask me if I minded that she fired it up.

The smoke dang near choked me, but I didn't say anything. I just kept talking.

"They will find a place on your property that is very non-invasive."

Wanda didn't seem to be very impressed. By now, she had her arms folded and had already smoked the Salem halfway down to the butt.

"What do you mean non-invasive?" she asked.

I tried not to smile, but I did. "That means we will do everything not to damage any of your property. Now I can't guarantee that, Mrs. Zimmerman.

There is always a risk, but it is a very small risk. The worst mess I have ever seen was just a sand pit about twenty yards long by twenty yards wide." We talked some more. I noticed that Wanda kept looking over at Bill. He was watching both of us. Finally, I saw him nod his head.

"I like you, Kid," Wanda said. "You're a good salesman. We've had several of your city slickers come out here and try to get us to sign a lease, but we wouldn't do it."

She took a long look at Bill. "But we're gonna do it with you. Are you gonna be around through all this or are you gonna be a ghost from now on?"

"Mrs. Zimmerman," I answered, "I'll be right here with you through all of it." I left the Zimmerman farm feeling good about myself. I had helped those folks. The drive back to the office was very enjoyable. I was fired up about telling my boss that we had finally broke through with the Zimmermans.

When I got back, I told him all about it, but he didn't seem nearly as enthusiastic as me. He was very solemn. It took me about ten minutes to tell the entire story. When I finished, he asked me to sit down. I had been standing the whole time.

"Kid," he said, "I have some bad news.

A bank bought our company yesterday.

They only had one stipulation to close the deal."

"What was the stipulation?" I asked.

He turned and looked out the window.

"Kid," he said, "I'm sorry. The only stipulation was that we terminate your employment from the company."

As I walked out the door, I couldn't separate the shock from the tears. I was devastated. I had just broken my promise to Wanda Zimmerman.

# CHAPTER FORTY - NINE

Macy Suggs was so mad she was tossin' her horns and pawin' the sod. Word travels fast in a small town, and she had just heard that her new husband had fired me for the second time. She had always liked me even though she didn't take me very seriously.

"Why did you do that?" she asked him.

"Haven't you done enough? Do you have to always get your way?"

Tom Wayne didn't seem to care. To him, I was just excess baggage in the overall plan.

"We don't need him in our organization," he replied. "Manpower is expensive. He wasn't getting the job done." Macy returned fire. "Baloney," she said.

"You just had to keep this stupid feud going. That's what it was, wasn't it?" Tom Wayne played it cool. He knew all he had to do was wait Macy's anger out a while and everything would be okay.

"Macy," he said, "you have to understand good business principles.

If someone isn't doing the job, you have to part ways with them. It wasn't personal. It was business."

Macy wasn't interested in hearing old movie quotes. She was madder than an old wet hen. It was embarrassing to her. All she wanted was some peace, and this incident gave her anything but that.

Tom Wayne tried to change the subject. "Macy," he said. "I picked up that necklace Runt gave Georgia off the bathroom floor this morning. I took it to the bank and put it in our safe deposit box. Those are real diamonds in that jewelry. Georgia's gonna lose 'em." Of course, that just made Macy even madder. "Now you're controlling my daughter's toys? Her father gave that to her. Don't you have a conscience?"

"Macy," he answered, "I just understand the value of money. That necklace will always be Georgia's. We just need to keep it safe. As a matter of fact, we need to put all that jewelry Runt gave her in our safe deposit box. I'll do it tomorrow."

Macy stormed away. She decided that she needed to go see her parents.

That was what she always did when she didn't get her way. When she got there, they talked and talked. They drank some coffee. They ate dinner and visited about old times. They watched Georgia play in the yard. Everything seemed so peaceful.

"Why do things have to be so complicated?" she thought to herself. "I just want to be happy."

Macy's dad had always been Runt's biggest critic. However, he preferred Runt over Tom Wayne Rhyner. It didn't matter how much money he had, Tom Wayne was very easy to dislike. Macy finally got around to telling her parents about what happened to me and what happened to the necklace.

Macy's dad became visibly upset.

"That doesn't surprise me," he said.

"There's a side to Tom Wayne that I've never liked."

Macy continued to talk and continued to ask questions. "Why?" she asked.

"Why do you think Tom Wayne is so hard on Kid? He never caused any problems, and he has nothing to do with all of our squabbles."

Macy's dad leaned back in his chair. He knew the answer, and he didn't mind telling Macy what it was.

"Macy, Darling," he said, "don't you understand? The best way for Tom Wayne to get back at Runt and Mule is to hurt Kid. It's the oldest trick in the book."

# CHAPTER FIFTY

Left the pickup and the cattle trailer, and I ran down to the bank. By then, Mule and Runt were sitting on some rocks staring out into the river.

It took us a good thirty minutes to compose ourselves.

"Kid," Runt finally said, "can you believe that truck and trailer hasn't fallen into the river by now?" I looked up at the bridge. The pickup was sitting at an angle with the back left tire just barely hanging on to the structure. You could see the stress it was creating. The cattle trailer was sitting pretty straight, though. I couldn't hear the cows. They were still quiet.

"Thanks, Runt," Mule said. "That was some quick thinking. I almost choked!"

"Well," Runt responded, "I couldn't just let you die up there hanging off the bridge. What would Mr. Derryberry say?"

The three of us sat there for a little while and enjoyed the fact that Mule wasn't dead. I was the one who finally broke the ice.

"What are we gonna do now?" I asked.

A minute went by before Runt broke the silence. "We need to say a prayer," he said. "God," this is Runt. We need to get across that bridge. Amen."

It kinda shocked me, and Mule wasn't impressed. "That was dumb, Runt," he said. "You don't know how to pray." Runt slowly made it to his feet. He was soaking wet and barefooted. He started to walk up the hill to the bridge. He had to be very careful that he didn't step on a sharp rock or a stick. Mule and I followed him.

The bridge was quietly swinging when we got up there. Very carefully, we approached the trailer and the pickup.

The cattle were still quiet.

The tow rope was hanging from the front of the truck down toward the water. Mule got down on his hands and knees and pulled it back up onto the floor of the bridge. He strung it out down the tracks. When he was finished getting it just the way he wanted, he looked at me and Runt.

Very carefully, Runt slid through the passenger door of the pickup. At any moment the whole thing could tip straight over into the river.

I didn't know what to do, so I just went to the back of the trailer and prepared to push. I was so scrawny that I didn't figure I would make much of a difference, but at least I was contributing a little.

Runt fired up the truck and slowly turned the steering wheel to point the tires back towards the tracks. All three of us took a deep breath.

Suddenly, Runt yelled out "GO!" Mule started pulling, and I started pushing.

We both gave it everything we had.

The pickup and trailer slowly started to move forward. Runt turned the truck to the right and got back onto the tracks.

Mule dropped the tow rope and jumped into the passenger seat of the truck. I stopped pushing and just watched. Runt drove the pickup and trailer across the river like a pro. He stopped safely on the other side of the bridge. It was very simple.

At that very moment, Mr. Derryberry drove around the corner and onto the bridge. He had to stop and let me walk to the other side. By the time we got to the cattle trailer, Mule had untied the tow rope and thrown it into the back of the pickup.

Mr. Derryberry got out of his truck.

He smiled as he approached us. "I was getting a little worried," he said. "You boys have been gone for a long time. I thought I had better check on you." Mule and Runt were soaking wet. "So, you boys decided to go swimming, huh?" Mr. Derryberry said. "I knew that's what you would do when you got to the river. Yeah, I knew that. You boys are wetter than a coyote in the rainy season."

Mr. Derryberry started laughing at his own joke. Right on cue, the cattle started mooing again. They wanted to tell him what they had just witnessed.

Me, Runt and Mule looked at each other. We all knew this story was so wild, nobody would ever believe us. At that moment, all three of us thought the same thing at the same time. This would always be our secret. It would be our secret forever.

# CHAPTER FIFTY - ONE

Tom Wayne Rhyner had now fired me twice. I was bitter as a mama cow with a sore teat. I wanted to find a way to get back at him, but I had no idea how to do it.

I sure had learned one thing, though. I wasn't gonna let somebody else control my income any longer. I decided to go into business for myself. I would do what I knew best.

My new company, Kid Fences, took off like a rocket. It was probably because I knew how to build any kind of fence you could imagine. Big fences, little fences, barb wire fences and see through fences, I built 'em all.

There wasn't much overhead. I knew where to get labor, and I knew where to get materials. The jobs came in easily.

People in Johnson County knew about my work with Mr. Derryberry. He had taught me well.

One day, Kid Fences decided to expand.
Runt told me about an old road that the county wanted to pave. It turned out to be an easy job. All I had to do was get on the bid list and submit my price. The next thing I knew, I got the contract.

I begged Runt to quit the county and go to work with me, but he wouldn't do it. Mule was the same way. He wanted no part of the fencing or paving business. It turned out that it wasn't hard at all, and Kid Fences had made a small fortune. At least, it was a small fortune to me.

We made 'em some great roads, too.

I figured there would be more work to come. My hunch was correct. Soon, we were focusing on building more roads than fences. There wasn't much competition. Before I knew it, we were bidding on re working highways.

Then one day the funniest thing happened. I was reading the county postings on what new construction was being considered, at first, I didn't see it. However, the second time through, it jumped out at me like a skinny armadillo. The old Johnson County Bridge was due to be torn down and replaced. I made up my mind right then and there that I was going to get that project.

Kid Fences had never done a bridge, so I had to do a lot of studying. Building roads wasn't much different than building fences. However, a bridge would be a lot different. The challenge engulfed me, and I went straight to work on it. What Mule, Runt and I went through there would never happen to anyone else again.

I couldn't wait to tell them about it.

They hadn't talked much for a couple of years. I thought this bridge project might be a good way to get the three of us back together again.

At first, neither of them was interested, but I was persistent. After a few calls, Mule started coming around a little, but Runt was more difficult. He just wasn't interested. Then one day out of the blue, he called me.

"Kid," Runt said, "you're right about that old bridge. I don't want anybody to ever have to cross that thing again. I'm glad you're rebuilding it."

I remember smiling as I listened to him on the other end of the phone line. Hopefully, we could not only fix the bridge but mend some of our own personal fences.

"When do you want to meet?" Runt asked.

"Well," I answered, "I'll be in Kansas City Friday night and Saturday morning. How 'bout we meet at the bridge Saturday night at 6:00 p.m. I'll bring the beer!"

"Who is gonna call Mule?" Runt asked.

"I'll do it," I replied. "I don't mind at all."

It got quiet on the other end of the line.

After a few seconds, Runt finally spoke.

"I think I should call him," he said.

"We'll see you Saturday night."

I remember how good I felt as I hung up the phone. Maybe, just maybe, the three of us were going to get back together again.

Runt did as he said he would do.

Immediately, he picked up the phone and called Mule.

After a couple of pleasantries, Runt brought up why he had called. "Mule," he said, "Kid wants to meet us out at the old Johnson County Bridge at 7:00 Friday night. He's gonna rebuild it, and he wants to get our opinion on the design. Can you make it?" Of course, Mule already knew about Kid's plan to fix the bridge. "Okay," he said. "I'll see you guys' Friday night."

"Good." Runt answered. "I'll see you on the north end of the bridge at seven."

Runt hung up the phone and smiled.

He took a swig of beer.

"Now," he said to himself, "I have another call to make."

# CHAPTER FIFTY - TWO

Tom Wayne Rhyner was on top of the world. It was 9:00 in the morning. A swearing in ceremony had been completed just a couple of hours ago. His first attempt at running for political office had been a success. He was the new mayor of Olathe, Kansas.

Strutting around town square was nothing new to him. He had been doing it his whole life. However, now he was the mayor. His wife, Macy, had opted not to share the success with him. She was pretty much put off by the whole thing. Tom Wayne's charm had run its course with her.

Tom Wayne made his way from patron to patron. He was wearing a new cowboy hat, a new pair of boots and a black sports coat. He was certain that he was now the biggest rooster in town.

But his joy didn't last for long. Bill Downing, a longtime resident of the town, was waiting for him at the corner pharmacy. "Mayor," Mr. Downing yelled "now that you're in-office, I bet we can get that tree cut down across the street from my house."

Tom Wayne looked at him in a funny way. He wasn't in the mood to worry about such trivial things like cutting down a tree on a day like this.

"Sure, Mr. Downing," Tom Wayne answered. "I'll get it taken care of first thing Monday morning."

However, Mr. Downing didn't stop there. "I would like for you to take a look at the daily schedule when my trash is picked up, too," he said. "I've been complaining about it for years, and nobody has ever done anything about it."

"Sure, sure," Tom Wayne answered.

"I'll look into it."

Tom Wayne picked up the pace of his walk. He needed to get away from Mr. Bill Downing. He turned the corner, and a lady approached him from across the street.

"Mr. Rhyner! Mr. Rhyner!" she yelled. "I need to talk to you. The city has messed up on my water bill again. You say I owe $186. I can't be using that much water.

I live by myself, and I only turn it on when necessary. I don't understand.

Can you look into it for me?"

Tom Wayne rolled his eyes before he spoke. "Yes, Ma'am," he said. "As soon as I get back to my office, I'll look into it."

"But Mr. Rhyner," the lady said, "I need help right now."

Before he could answer, another man approached him. "Mayor," the man said, "I have a pothole in my alley so big it will swallow a car. I want it fixed." Tom Wayne didn't even acknowledge him. He just turned and started walking. The lady who didn't like her water bill followed him. "Mr. Rhyner," she continued "I need help!" Tom Wayne kept on walking.

He picked up the pace, turned the corner and disappeared into City Hall.

Soon he was in the sanctuary of his new office. He sat down in the mayor's chair.

He leaned back to enjoy the moment.

Suddenly, there was a knock on the door. Tom Wayne looked up to see who it was. There stood a man wearing a white cowboy hat. He was also wearing a badge.

"Mr. Tom Wayne Rhyner?" he asked.

Tom Wayne nodded his head.

"My name is Detective Carl James. I represent the Kansas Department of Justice. Do you own the Olathe City Bank?"

"Of course, I do," Tom Wayne answered. "What's this all about?"

"Well," Carl James answered, "this is a legal document to search your bank for stolen jewelry. We have reason to believe it is in your possession at the bank."

Tom Wayne Rhyner's jaw almost hit the floor. "I have no idea what you are talking about." he said.

Detective Carl James looked at him for a few seconds and finally answered.

"Well, Mr. Rhyner," he said, "the state of Kansas thinks that you DO know what I'm talking about."

# CHAPTER FIFTY - THREE

The trip to the bank was a long one for Tom Wayne Rhyner. Just yesterday, he was on top of the world. He had been elected mayor of his hometown. Today, the authorities wanted to search his bank for stolen property.

Detective Carl James was an ornery old coot. He was almost six foot four, and he probably weighed close to three hundred pounds. His flat top burr haircut was intimidating, and his big, round eyeglasses were spooky.

Tom Wayne got to the bank and found Carl James waiting for him in the foyer.

Carl was holding a document.

"Sign here," he said to Tom Wayne.

"This warrant is for a particular piece of jewelry. I have a picture of it right here." Carl flipped the page over and sure enough there was a picture of a diamond. Tom Wayne recognized it immediately.

"That diamond was a gift to my daughter. I had no idea that it was stolen," Tom Wayne said feverishly. "I don't know what to say."

Carl James closed his right eye and opened his left eye really wide. The weird look on his face scared Tom Wayne.

"Let's go in and take a look," Carl said.

You could cut the tension with a knife.

Tom Wayne's day was getting ready to get worse.

Of course, Tom Wayne knew right where to go. It was in his safe deposit box. A thought suddenly hit him.

"There are several diamonds in there," he thought.

"Runt did it to me again!"

Tom Wayne pulled out the safe deposit box and opened it. Sure enough, there were several diamonds and jewels glistening at the both of them. Tom Wayne noticed that Carl seemed to enjoy what he was doing. He looked at Tom Wayne and smacked his lips in a weird way.

Carl was careful not to touch the evidence. He put on a pair of disposable gloves. Slowly, he started poking through the diamonds with some kind of a probe. It didn't take long for him to find the one in the picture.

Carl picked it up with a pair of tweezers and looked at it closely.

Next, he looked at the picture. It was a match. Slowly, he placed the diamond in a small plastic bag. When he was finished, he started reading Tom Wayne his rights. Next came the handcuffs.

After that, Carl James escorted Tom Wayne Rhyner right out the front door of the Olathe City Bank. He did it in front of everybody in town.

# CHAPTER FIFTY - FOUR

Later that night, mule drove up to the north end of the old Johnson County Bridge. He did it just as he was instructed.

Mule got out of his car and started looking around. He was the only person there.

"Surely," he thought. "I didn't get my days mixed up."

A few minutes later, an old pickup drove up at the other end of the bridge. That was the south end. Mule recognized the pickup immediately. It belonged to Runt.

Slowly, Mule and Runt started walking towards each other. When they got about a hundred feet or so apart, they both stopped walking at the same time.

The weather was very calm and mild, and there was no wind.

The two of them stared at each other for a couple of minutes. Finally, Runt broke the ice.

"Mule, you know I'm the one who robbed all those people," he said. "We don't have to pretend anymore." Mule didn't say anything for a few seconds. Finally, he knew he had to say something.

"Well," he said, "I wasn't a hundred percent sure before you admitted to it, but I guess I know now."

Runt smiled, but Mule didn't change expressions at all.

"I'm not turning myself in," Runt yelled. "You and me can just settle it right here on the bridge."

Mule knew what he meant, but he thought he had better ask to be sure.

"What are you talking about?" he asked.

That was when Runt reached down and took his .22 out of his right boot.

He pointed it straight to the ground. Of course, he knew Mule always carried a loaded gun.

Mule started trying to talk him out of all this nonsense.

"Drop that gun on the bridge," he pleaded. "Neither one of us wants this!" But Runt wouldn't say or do anything.

He just stood there, so Mule tried again.

"Runt," he said. "Drop the gun. You need to just turn around and go on home. We can settle this another way." It didn't work. Runt just stood there.

"How do we do this, Mule?" he asked.

"I've always wondered."

"We're not gonna do anything," Mule answered. "You're gonna put that gun down, and we're gonna,"

"We're gonna do what?" Runt interrupted.

Mule didn't know what to say. He hadn't thought it that far through.

"I'll never get out of prison, Mule," Runt said. "You know that. I'm not up for it. You're the only person who knows. We need to settle this today."

"If you shoot me, everybody's gonna know it was you," Mule responded.

Runt laughed. "No, they won't," he said.

"People know there are a lot of guys who want to kill you. They'll just think it was another one of those wanna be's. It doesn't matter anyway. I'll be long gone before they find you."

Mule stared at him. "What if I shoot you?" he asked.

Runt stared back. "Well," he said, "I guess I'll just have to take my chances."

Another minute went by before Runt spoke again. Mule was content just to wait him out.

"How 'bout we count to five?" Runt asked. "On five, it's showtime."

Mule was not amused. "This is stupid, Runt," he said. "Let's go home."

"One" Runt yelled.

Ten seconds passed before he yelled again. "Two."

After another ten seconds, he said

"Three." His voice seemed to crack a little.

Mule reached over with his left hand and unsnapped his holster, so he could pull his gun.

"Four," Runt continued. Mule Archer and Runt Suggs looked each other right in the eyes.

"Five!" Runt yelled. The crack of the gunshot sounded like a lightning bolt.

# CHAPTER FIFTY - FIVE

The drive to the Kansas State Penitentiary was long and quiet. It had been almost six months since the sentencing. Mule and I had put this trip off long enough.

Of course, Mule had all kinds of benefits in the law enforcement business. I just hung around with him, and they let me through all the gates and bars and doors and such. For some reason, nobody seemed to be concerned about me being dangerous.

They finally parked us in a little cubicle. Mule pulled up a chair for me.

That was really nice of him, but it made the seating arrangement awkward.

We both crowded into the cubicle and looked through the window. There was a little table with a chair on the other side. It was impersonal and cold.

After a few minutes, a guard walked Runt through a door. He was wearing orange coveralls, and he had shackles on both his ankles and wrists. His noticeable limp really bothered me. He looked harmless, but convicted armed robbers don't get any exception to the rules.

Runt didn't look at us until he sat down and took a deep breath. Finally, he gazed right into my eyes. After a few seconds, he turned to Mule.

We waited for him to speak first, but he didn't say anything for at least a minute. Finally, he spoke.

"What took you so long?" he asked. "I thought you guys would have busted me out of here by now!"

Mule leaned back in his chair and put his hands over his mouth. He had to hide that he had almost busted out laughing.

I decided to ask a question. "How you doing, Runt?"

He scowled at me. "Food's terrible here, Kid," he said. "Next time you come, try to sneak in a Big Mac for me."

"How's your leg?" I asked.

"They say it'll get better," he answered.

A full minute went by before anybody said anything else. Finally, it was Runt who broke the ice.

"Mule," he asked, "why didn't you just kill me like you did those other guys?" Mule leaned over in his chair and put his elbows on his knees. He looked like he might cry.

"I've never been near as good a shot as everybody gives me credit," he answered

"Well, that wasn't my plan," Runt said.

"You were supposed to do me in just like you did the old farmer and the guy at the carnival."

"Well, it just didn't happen that way," Mule responded.

"You sure pulled one over on Tom Wayne," I said. "That was really smart."

Runt squirmed in his seat. "I didn't plan that," he said. "He should have known not to put those diamonds in his bank. That jewelry was for Georgia. It wasn't for him."

Mule perked up. He had his own questions.

"So, you didn't turn Tom Wayne in?" he asked.

Runt rolled his eyes and smiled at us.

"No," he answered. "I would never do that, Sir!"

Mule and I looked at each other. Both of us knew that every time he said "Sir" he was lying. We had heard him do it for years.

Nobody said anything for a few seconds. Finally, Runt raised his head and started talking again.

"Yeah, I did it!" he said. "But I couldn't let somebody go to prison for something I did, not even Tom Wayne Rhyner. I guess I'm a crook, but I don't frame people."

Until that moment, Mule and I were just like everybody else in town. We weren't sure if Runt had planned the whole thing or not, but now we knew the truth. Of course, he did it.

"Why did you fake the gunfight, Runt?" Mule asked.

Runt was quick with an answer.

"Mule," he said, "when those guys challenged you, you killed 'em. I questioned you about it both times. I just figured you would do me in, too.

You didn't, though. You shot me in the dang leg!"

"I'm sorry," Mule mumbled.

We sat there in the quiet for a minute or so. All three of us knew we were almost out of time.

"Revenge and hate are terrible things,"

Runt said. "It's no way to live. You guys remember that."

I couldn't help myself. I had to get an answer to one specific question. "Runt," I asked, "why did you rob all those people? You knew that was wrong." Runt rubbed his bad leg. "Well, Kid," he answered, "Mr. Derryberry used to say that he never saw a good farmer who didn't love farming. I guess the same thing applies to me. I never saw a good thief who didn't love stealing!"

I guess in some odd way his answer gave me and Mule what people call closure.

"Do they have any pain killers they can give you for your leg?" I asked.

Runt stared at me before he answered.

"Kid," he said, "there ain't no medicine for this kind of pain."

Suddenly, the guard walked up behind him. "It's time to go, men," he said quietly.

"You were supposed to kill me, Mule!"

Runt said abruptly.

Mule was quick with an answer. "I saved your life instead, just like how you saved my life at the bridge!"

It was very intense. The guard decided to step into the conversation.

"Runt," he said, "the men are waiting for you."

Runt stood up. As he did, the guard handed him a bible. Runt started to shuffle away, but the guard wanted to tell us something.

"Runts got quite a following round here," he said.

Mule and I were dumbfounded. "What do you mean?" I asked.

"He leads the prison worship services." the guard said. "He's the best I've ever seen!"

After that comment, Mule and I just stared at each other in disbelief. Runt never ceased to amaze us.

Mule and I went back outside the prison gates, but neither of us wanted to leave. The walk back to the parking lot was very quiet. We dropped the back gate of my truck and sat down. The view of the prison was impressive. The sun was slowly setting behind it.

After a few minutes of odd silence, Mule finally spoke. "He'll never get out of there, Kid. He confessed to almost a hundred-armed robberies. We couldn't ever catch him. I doubt if we would have ever pinned any of them on him.

He was the best thief I've ever seen."

"Did it ever occur to you that he was robbing people?" I asked.

Mule thought for a moment. "Yeah," he answered. "I figured it was him, but I was never sure. I followed him around for Tom Wayne Rhyner."

Mule wiped away a tear. "But," he continued, "I just never.... It just never all came together. I guess I always just gave him the benefit of the doubt." I figured that I should say something, so I did. "Well, I never had a clue. Now, I knew there was some odd behavior, but I never thought he was the Courteous Crook."

A couple of minutes elapsed with nothing said. It was Mule who broke the silence again. "Kid," he said, "do you think us being such good friends all these years was a good thing?" The question threw me off guard. I had to think for a few moments before I answered.

"Yeah, it was a good thing," I answered.

"I'm closer to you and Runt than I am my own family."

# CHAPTER FIFTY - SIX

Mr. Derryberry shut the door to the pickup before he spoke. "Okay, boys," he said, "now, be careful. You've done a good job, so far. Let's get these cattle to the pasture."

"Yes, Sir," I answered. "We'll be really careful."

I fired up the ignition and put the pickup in gear. Away we went.

"Whoo Hoo!" Runt yelled. "We barely made it before the old man drove up on us! That was something else, wasn't it?" He laughed and laughed and laughed.

Mule wasn't quite as enthusiastic.

"Let's just finish this job and go home," he said. "I've had enough excitement for the day."

We only had to drive four miles. When we arrived, Mule jumped out to open the gate. As I passed through, Runt reached over with his left foot and hit the gas pedal. The truck and trailer took off like we were gonna leave Mule behind.

Mule closed the gate and started chasing us. Finally, I stopped the truck. I knew Mule would be furious.

"Why did you do that, Kid?!" he yelled.

"I'm sorry, Mule. I'm sorry!" I answered.

That was Runt's chance to say something smart. "Dang Kid! You can't drive worth nothin'!"

I just stared at him. Of course, he acted like he didn't do anything wrong.

Mule jumped in the truck, and we took off again. Soon, we were at our destination. I stopped the truck. Mule and Runt were all but fighting to set the cattle free from the trailer.

"Yo! Move!" Mule barked at them. Soon, the cattle were roaming all over the pasture. The three of us watched them.

The experience of success felt great.

"I'm sure glad I said that prayer back at the bridge," Runt said.

"Well, that was a pretty bad prayer,
Runt," I answered.

I remember that I was still mad at him, but I'll never forget the look he gave me before he spoke.

"Well, Kid," he said, "it worked, didn't it?"

# ABOUT THE AUTHOR

**GERALD BRENCE. OLD MONEY** is his third novel. His first novel, *Ox in the Culvert*, is a historical fiction story about the California Gold Rush. His second novel, *Agent 49*, is also a historical fiction novel. It is about a master thief who is recruited by the government to spy on a plot to commit one of the greatest crimes of the century. His first book, *The 70-30-Split,* is non-fiction. It is about high school football.